this
is
all
we
know

Robin Anne Ettles

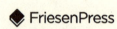 FriesenPress

One Printers Way
Altona, MB R0G 0B0
Canada

www.friesenpress.com

Cover mural art by Eelco van den Berg @iameelco
Used with permission.
Photographed by Mathieu Léger @mlegerart

www.rae-creative.org
@surrealist_rodeo

ISBN
978-1-03-831073-6 (Hardcover)
978-1-03-831072-9 (Paperback)
978-1-03-831074-3 (eBook)

1. FICTION, LITERARY

Distributed to the trade by The Ingram Book Company

Contents

The Last Supperware

Last one, last one. This is to be the last one.

Debra had missed the last Tupperware party, which was supposed to be the last one. But now this was it.

This is it.

She sat in her parked vehicle for a moment. She took in Ashley's Cape Cod home with the lights on in every single room, illuminating each window as if it were Christmas, except it was early September. Excessive, even for 1983.

"Debbie!" glowed Ashley as they met at the door, her face electric with excitement and makeup. "It's been so long!"

So long...

"So long, I know!" Debra took off her blazer and followed Ashley to the kitchen, where their high school circle of friends sat on tall stools around the island. "Hi everyone."

Carol and Susan waved in greeting, their mouths too full of canapés to say hello properly. Jess hung to the side, eyeing the blender and the perfectly arranged display of ingredients and alcohol soon to be combined into an easier time. She turned and greeted Debra warmly. Debra appreciated this, but felt a heaviness coming from her friend as well.

What happened to you. You were a bit like this last time, too.

"Salad bites, deviled ham, and other goodies before Bobbie arrives!" Ashley waved her arm broadly across the spread of finger foods, displayed and served exclusively in Tupperware. "I can't WAIT to see what she's got this time."

Everyone talked about how Bobbie was new. Ashley had discovered her at Leanne's last Tupperware party and couldn't wait to introduce her to everyone. Bobbie had such good ideas around recipes for each piece, and such a wicked presentation style. The girls were going to LOVE her.

The basement door opened, and Ashley's husband Mike appeared. "Forgot the beer," he said with mock regret. He smirked while looking over his wife's friends. Debra turned to the wall prior to rolling her eyes.

"Michael! You get your beer and get back down there to your poker game!" Ashley drew him in for a kiss while his eyes rested on Jess's back. He turned to Debra.

"Debra the Zebra," he drawled in a terrible British accent, reviving her high school nickname from a place she had hoped it would remain forever lost. "How's the Lady-in-Law? Jack and Steve letting you take some good cases?"

Idiot.

Her partners were well aware that she could whip their asses in a court of law, blindfolded and with her hands tied behind her back. They never hesitated to hand her the big winners.

Maybe a little too often.

Debra smiled. "Jack and Steve are more than pleased with my billing," she said, carrot stick in hand and the intent to shut this down quickly.

Ashely grabbed the reins. "Downstairs!" she pointed, baring her teeth in the guise of a smile. Too much attention was drifting the wrong way.

Mike and his case of beer disappeared. Ashley approached the blender. Jess stepped aside but did not go far. "We're drinking strawberry daiquiris, people!" rang Ashley. "Are we good with that?"

Carol and Susan, still munching, managed a "Yeah, sure!"

Ashley paused and turned to Debra, her voice loaded with condescension. "It's not scotch, though, Deb. That's more your thing, right? You okay with daiquiris, with the rest of us?"

Debra. Not Deb. Not Debbie. DEBRA.

"Can't wait," lied Debra with a smile, although there was truth in the scotch statement. There was also truth to the butterflies she experienced each time she bought a bottle from the specialty liquor store.

Strange how it always seemed to be the same girl working. How they could talk a long time about scotch, about how their brothers bragged up their own selections but seemed to truly know nothing, about their favourite hiking trails from coast to coast, about how they had both played flute in high school band but hadn't touched an instrument since.

She turned her attention back to her friends. "And how are everyone's husbands and kids?"

This set into motion a welcome period of silence for Debra. Her friends delighted in talking about their husbands and their homes and their pools and their trips to Florida and their kids and their kids' tennis lessons.

Last time. This is the last time I'll have to sit through this.

She noticed that she didn't have to summon sincerity while listening to Jess's update. Jess's kids were fun, and did funny things, and weren't growing up too fast. Meanwhile, Jess poured her third daiquiri as the others finished their first.

Ashley hit the blender again and the mixtape hit Duran Duran.

I won't see them for a long time.

Debra tried to be present and enjoy what was left of the girls she had known in high school, a time before adulthood and adultery had kicked in.

She found maintaining both presence and enjoyment too effortful, and she excused herself to the washroom. "Use the ensuite in the master, Debbie!" shouted Ashley over the blender. "We just redecorated the whole thing! I want a full report on what you think of the colours."

"Debra."

"What?" asked Ashley. She stopped the blender.

Debra didn't think Ashley had heard. The room was still and silent but for the Duran Duran. "Debra," she repeated, sipping her daiquiri. "That's my name."

Ashley snorted and turned to face Debra, unappreciative of the amendment. Just as Ashley opened her shiny, angry lips to retaliate, Debra proclaimed, "Debra the Zebra!" with a perfect accent, grinning and running her hands through her hair where the trademark white stripes had been for the duration of her graduation year. The tide of transaction turned. All laughed in delight except Ashley, who managed a delayed "ha." She turned back to the blender, her shoulders tense.

In the theme of stripes, the bathroom had been painted entirely in diagonal ones, alternating vibrant green and dark pink. It was hideous. Debra dried her hands on a monogrammed towel, checked her toned-down version of everyone else's makeup, and did what ninety-five percent of guests do in someone else's ensuite: go through the drawers and cabinets.

None of the contents were remarkable or scandalous. There were many colours of nail polish. Sucrets, Anacin, Vicks VapoRub. A sleep aid, which was slightly more interesting, but also well known as a placebo. Unsatisfied, Debra left the bathroom and quietly opened the doors to the walk-in closet.

She snapped on the light and took a good look around both sides. His and Hers. It was much more orderly than she expected. Ashley was all about the show, but the state of one's living room rarely reflects that of one's bedroom closet. So much money spent on clothes here; then again, so much money spent on everything. Debra delicately brushed her hand across a long rack of shirts and dresses. There was a hat tree in the shadows behind them, and a familiar shape caught Debra's eye. She parted the clothing, illuminating her deceased mother's synchronized swimming cap.

That's not what I'm seeing.

She turned her head away, then back.

Is it?

She reached in and clasped the 1950s-style cap. She turned its faded flowered exterior inside out to see her mother's initials, broken by time and chlorine, in the rubber underneath.

Her body went still with shock. It belied the backdraft of possessiveness, violation, and anger that rushed through her. A sharp wave of guilt landed for not having noticed the cap was missing from her own bedroom closet.

For how long?

Their families were friends, had hung out together. Ashley's mother had never been on the synchronized swim team. It made no sense.

Debra folded the cap in her hand and went to put it in the pocket of her blazer before realizing she had removed the blazer when she arrived at the party. A resentful second thought guided her hand and the cap back to its dark post in someone else's home. She stepped out of the closet and pushed the doors shut. She took a few deep breaths in front of the full-length mirror, righted her posture, and descended to the kitchen.

"And??" asked Ashley immediately.

"Breathtaking," returned Debra.

The doorbell rang. "All right!" cried Ashley. "Everyone to the living room—it's time for Bobbie and Tupperware!"

Bobbie and Tupperware erupted through the doorway like a manic Fourth of July parade. "Turn up the music, girls," Bobbie shouted, "it's time to dance!" She and Ashley danced their way up the hall. Bobbie's outfit was classic matchy-matchy baggy Esprit in a violent shade of violet. Her bangs were high, her glasses gargantuan, her voice theatrical and driven. She gave excessive compliments and asked questions, allowing no space for response. She was far more about entertainment than Tupperware. The show was grand.

She must be making a pile of money.

Debra had arrived with zero intention of purchasing. She held to it. Yes, she had the deviled egg tray. No thank you, she didn't need freezer storage, or anything for the kids' lunches. The others gushed and giggled and spent, especially Jess.

Poor Jess. Does no one else see this.

Something was odd about the glitz and glamour of the presenter. Debra enjoyed a good show but had never experienced this. So over the top. So loud. So … dressed up. Within her non-stop monologue, Bobbie imitated the husband of the host from the last party. Everyone but Debra doubled over with laughter and delight.

Debra cocked her head sideways. The voice was not of a woman doing an excellent impression of a man—it was the sound of one man imitating another. Debra spent her days in courtrooms listening to all manner of voices giving testimony, to all spectrums of inflection, stress, flatness, depth, truth, lies. She now saw the layers of foundation on Bobbie's face, the shaved hands, the Adam's apple under the high-necked shirt as she … (he?) wheeled to and from the display table.

Does no one else see THIS?

Debra felt strange and fascinated. The presenter before her was no longer the one who had flounced down the hallway twenty minutes earlier. This was a whole new person. It was hard to process. It was electric.

Bobbie.

Bobby.

Jess knocked some pieces off the table, sending them to the ground with the spilled plastic clatter that only Tupperware can make. Debra's focus snapped back to the room.

It's over.

"Time to get you home," she said, stepping in to steady a teetering Jess. She handed her over to Ashley, who nodded quietly but clearly in agreement: a mess would not be made of this event. "Get her ready, Ashley, I'm just going to run to the bathroom one last time before I head out."

Debra grabbed her blazer and raced up the stairs to the master bedroom closet. Her heart jumped as she folded the swimming cap and tucked it into her pocket. Anger surged; she wasn't done. Her eyes rested on Mike's rack of ties. She chose an expensive one. She liked the feel of it. It had a bold paisley pattern in pastel blue and pink. She closed the closet doors and faced her reflection in the full-length mirror, holding the tie up to her neck. It suited her. Its soft weight felt like something she was always meant to hold. Satisfied and excited, she placed the tie in her free pocket. She turned away from her reflection and then from everyone else as she guided Jess out the door.

5B

Translation of Eric's dialogue is available at the end of this passage.

Montréal, circa 2005.

Daniel graduates from high school. He is accepted into Concordia for Political Science and moves into a quintessential brick box apartment with a wrought iron spiral staircase.

It is not a student building. It is a fair distance from campus. It was what he could find in late summer, well after Moving Day, on account of procrastinating.

The brick box is slowly crumbling on the outside from decades of winter and neglect, and rotting on the inside from decades of boiled meals and disregard. Bland shades of paint are applied poorly, here and there, now and then. By contrast, patches of colour shout from the window box gardens of two of the seventeen units. Actual human shouting is abundant.

He doesn't care. He is away from home. He is away from his helicopter parents. He is away from his older sister's shadow, first cast over him from her position as an overachieving yet badass valedictorian, then as a doctor.

He is away from his twin brother's shadow, the long omnipresent shadow of a twin brother who went missing without a trace when they were three years old.

7

Daniel doesn't love Political Science, but he is decent at debate and has a good memory. These assets have kept him afloat academically and assured the minimal university entry requirements. He hopes to "find himself," although he has zero clue as to who he might be looking for.

Despite or perhaps because of what happened to his brother, Daniel is from an upbringing of there-is-nothing-wrong. He has had no fights on his hands, literal or proverbial. He was never cornered or neglected. There were no glaring successes or lags in any of his milestones or activities. Learning to read and learning to play baseball occurred with equal averageness. He has no particular leanings or edge. He prefers fish to meat, pop to rock, girls to boys. He works hard enough. He plays hard enough. He sleeps well.

Until he doesn't.

There has been no defining event to his insomnia since moving to Montréal. He finds himself getting home a bit later than usual a couple of nights a week, having joined an evening improv club to shore up his debate skills. Perhaps this threw his circadian rhythm.

Now that he walks up his street from the bus station at a later hour, he develops a new relationship with his building. At night, it is almost pretty. The wear in the brick is invisible. The outdoor lights feature the striking sculpture of the staircase. Most neighbours leave their curtains or blinds open.

On Tuesdays, the lady in the second-floor corner unit wears pink pyjamas. On Thursdays, she wears lime green. She seems to have a daughter in her early teens, but this person has only appeared in frame once, so it's difficult to confirm. A guy in one of the basement units plays video games with no lights on. He exists as an outline of head, torso, and elbows within a haze of weed smoke that takes on the colour of the flashing screen. Glancing into the adjacent basement apartment, Daniel finally pairs the image of a flesh-and-blood man with the booming, obnoxious twang he has heard from the unit directly below his own for the last three months. The window is permanently open. The voice carries both inside and out.

The man is big in every way. Daniel can't get over the bigness of him. He is overweight and has a large head. His hair is sparse but curly and unkempt, so it's also big. He wears undershirts or NASCAR shirts with the sleeves cut off. His arms are white and bulbous. He gestures widely with them. He talks the same amount, no matter how many other people are in the tiny living space. They are almost always the same people. He has a twang: Outer Montréal. Vieux-Longueuil, perhaps.

In late October, the temperature starts to drop and the man begins to wear an oversized yet snug Canadiens jersey. He wears it every day. A warm front pushes through and he wears a purple Budweiser T-shirt, brand new. He remains unwashed, sweaty, and loud in his new T-shirt with the sleeves cut off.

The man's name is Éric.

Daniel finds himself transfixed, fascinated.

A few weeks go by. Nothing changes in Daniel's campus life except he misses a few early morning classes because he can. He spends time outdoors in the evenings, discreetly watching, sometimes from the bus stop bench, sometimes from the top of the slide in a run-down playground across the street. Nothing changes in the building, aside from more people wearing long-sleeved items. As of early November, a third-floor window goes dark, and remains dark.

While still fascinated by the vibrating, meaty pile of Éric's physical form, Daniel begins to gather other details. There is a lot of drinking, nightly. It can take several days before the table and countertop are cleared of cans. The window is permanently open because Éric and his people are career smokers. No one changes their clothes much. Someone drinks as much Diet Pepsi as the others drink beer.

Éric yells at the TV. Less so as the evening wears on, because his yelling becomes directed at a woman who appears to be his sister. She is a shorter, slightly more compact version of him with piles of thick, dyed black hair. She is covered in disorganized tattoos and never wears a sweater. He complains about his pension; she complains about him complaining about it. She wishes she had a pension so she wouldn't have to spend the rest of her life working as a cleaner at the strip mall at the edge of their quartier.

« Mais mon chèque, là, mon chèque, ch'devrais l'avoir sans être rappelé tout l'temps au pied comme un astie d'chien. Me suis faite suivre, câlisse! Deux gars dans leu' char noir. Ch'les ai vus à 'a fin août, ch'les voyais, tsé. Crisse de taches à marde, deux girafes dans leu' polo de golf, tabarnak.

Quelle astie d'niaiserie, suivre un gars parce qu'y reçoit un chèque. En tout cas y'en ont vu un se pogner le cul pas rien qu'un peu, haha! » Éric re-creates this scene; all laugh but the sister, Marie-Ève. One man chokes on his own smoky phlegm for some time, spits into a nearby beer can. His name is Kevin.

Daniel has never experienced anything like this. He looks down at his own golf shirt.

Chèque. Bien-être social? Rente d'invalidité? Daniel cannot equate this piece of substantial human real estate with the word "invalid."

What was this man like as a baby? As a little boy? Daniel imagines a fat kid with messy blonde hair, not capable of listening, controlled only by the promise of snacks. His next picture of Éric is at CÉGEP. Éric gets expelled for repeated vandalism and refusing to smoke off school property. No one expresses concern that he is ruining his future or will not reach his full potential. Éric is his own person. He has exercised some control over his life and destiny.

Daniel unconsciously clenches his hands from the cold. He finds himself barely able to move. It is 1:30 a.m.

November forces him inside. On a rare night that he agrees to go for a drink after improv club, he meets a girl at the pub. They have beer, more beer, some tequila. They wind up back at his apartment. The next morning, they lie naked with the sheets off. The temperature in his unit, over which he has no control, is always searing. He tries to force some chips down as the woman wakes to the crunching, rolls toward him, and reaches for the bag. She asks what it's like to live in this building, this neighbourhood.

Daniel starts by talking about the long bus rides and transfers, but quickly moves on to Éric. He doesn't mention any of the other tenants. He forgets his churning stomach as he describes the scene one floor below. She rises, dresses, thanks him for the night, and leaves. He realizes they haven't exchanged numbers. His singular goal is now to close his eyes to sleep off the nausea.

That evening, he wakes in a better state. He bundles up and crosses the street to sit atop the slide. He catches up on Éric, Kevin, and Marie-Ève. Florent is there tonight as well.

« Chris-no-balls, là, gardien de marde. Y vaut rien, câlisse! Moé si ch'avais son cash, mon gars … les femmes que ch'me pognerais! Florent, t'es fou crisse, Paméla Anderson est à moé, pas à toé. Mais a doit avoir des soeurs, tsé, ou au moins des amies chéarleedar, peut-être toute une équipe d'amies chéarleedar, ééééé, là on parle »

By Christmas break, Daniel has gained 30 pounds. He cleans himself up and changes out of his sweats before his parents pick him up. Their features expand into surprise and disconcertion at his appearance. They exchange looks in the car more than once over the course of the drive. He finally pats his belly and tells them it's the Frosh Thirty, and they all laugh superficially. Each day of the break, he spills out of the clothes he had brought with him to school. He feels like an imposter in them. He is the only child home for Christmas this year.

Christmas morning, he receives a fat bike. His parents had decided on the gift without knowledge of his change in stature. They make this sinking connection as he opens it. Their intention was for him to enjoy winter trail biking and to provide an option for getting around the city. The moment is awkward. Pre-university Daniel feels a twinge of excitement and pleasure at the bike, and a desire for his parents to feel happy about their gift to him. Éric's neighbour Daniel can't imagine riding it. Ever.

Éric's neighbour Daniel doesn't exist to Éric. Daniel has never realized this until now.

Daniel returns to his apartment. He leaves the bike outside overnight. He leaves it outside overnight again. It is stolen. The next evening, he begins to knock on doors. He is selective. He chooses the darkened unit on third, the unit with the senior couple who can barely hear or see, and Éric's.

Daniel knocks, shaking with anticipation. He chews his lips. He teeters rapidly from one foot to the other. He gives his head a quick toss to get the hair out of his eyes, and wills himself to stillness.

The door opens. It is Marie-Ève who answers. He plants his feet so as to not be crushed by the wall of heat, smoke, sweat, and garbage that pushes out. It is revolting. Marie-Ève is shorter than he perceived. In the background, so is Éric.

« Ouin? » she barks. He explains the bike theft, asks if they saw anything.

« On est au sous-sol, t'attends qu'on voit quoé? »

Éric is in a loud, talking-over-each-other exchange with Kevin about the mayor. Marie-Ève interrupts to ask Éric about the bike. Éric looks at Daniel with disgust. His eyes are hard and unreceptive. « T'as laissé ton bicyc' déhors, mon gars, astie d'débile. Essaye-toé avec le 5B en face, c'te gars-là dort jamais, y'é ku chon Xbox vingt-quatre chept. » Éric turns back to Kevin. « Ké-vun, si tu crois que les politi-chiens vont donner un bréék su'es impôts, t'es fou raide. Nous autres on a déjà quasiment rien a'ec notre chèque, c'est l'enfer partout au pays, 'sti! »

Marie-Ève shuts the door.

Daniel's emotions are visceral and conflicting. His thoughts race. *Why did I find this man fascinating? How much time have I spent watching these people? My bike's gone. I feel like shit. I look like shit.* He turns to the pocked presswood door across the hall. His eyes land on the grimy italicized plate characters, installed unevenly at waist level. 5B.

He is unable to knock, or even approach. He begins to climb the stairs to his own apartment.

It occurs to him that Éric has somehow noticed something about someone beyond his own four-walled universe, even if only a small detail about his immediate neighbour. That night, Daniel puts on his hat and winter coat, and heads across to the top of the slide. His focus this time is on the window of 5B, and the young man contained within another set of four small walls and the various levels of his Sony-driven worlds.

The young man is also somewhat overweight and unkempt. There is less smoke effect than usual; perhaps he is between joints. Twitching his head sideways, perhaps in a moment of strategizing or memory, his absent gaze is framed by the window. He cannot see Daniel.

Daniel, however, comes undone as he views his mirror image.

« Mais mon chèque, là, mon chèque … »

"So my cheque, you know, my cheque, I should be able to get that without having to heel like a dog all the time. They tailed me, for fuck's sake! Two guys in a black car. End of August, that's when I saw them, yeah.

Goddamn pieces of shit, two giraffes in their golf shirts. Fuckin' ridiculous, following a man on benefits around just to watch him whack off. Well if that's what they came to see, I fuckin' gave them something to see, haha!"

« Chris-no-balls, là, gardien de marde … »

"Chris-no-balls, what a piece of shit goalie. He's not worth fuck-all! But if I had his cash, man, the women I'd get. Florent, you're nuts, Pamela Anderson, she's mine, not yours. But she must have sisters, you know, or at least cheerleader friends, maybe a whole team of cheerleader friends, hey, now we're talkin'"

« On est au sous-sol, t'attends qu'on voit quoé? »

"We live in the basement, what is it you think we can see?"

« T'as laissé ton bicyc' déhors, mon gars … »

"You left a bike outside, you fuckin' idiot. Try 5B across the hall, that guy never sleeps, he's on his X-Box 24/7 … Kevin, if you think politicians are gonna give people a break on their taxes, you're insane. We hardly get anything with our cheque already, the whole country's gone to hell, for Christ's sake!"

Dear Brenda

Dear Brenda,

Your weeds are very bad on your lawn. They attract many bees and my daughter is allergic. I have to make her play in our small backyard. She does not understand and she is unhappy many days. If you do not want to use chemicals, please at least mow more often.

   - Julie

Dear Julie,

Thank you for writing with your concerns about my lawn. The weeds are dandelions. They feed the bees, who, as you probably know, are essential to plant life and therefore to our food, oxygen, and ecosystem. I'm sorry your daughter is allergic. I happen to be allergic to your pesticides and have to spend more time in my own small backyard than I would like. Maybe you could try to find a friendlier solution. I will try to cut the front lawn a little more often.

   Brenda

Dear Brenda,

I saw you mowed the lawn a couple of weeks ago after the first email. Thank you but the lawn needs to be mowed again. My little girl played out front only for a few days, now she is in the backyard all the time again. Does not seem fair. Summer is short, kids need to be outside with air and space to run while on break from school. Thank you for being helpful the first time.

    -J

Dear Julie,

As you know, because you watched me the whole time from your window, I have just mowed the lawn again as per your request. Hopefully your child can enjoy playing out front for a while. I too would like to spend more time in my front yard, but while you are still treating your lawn with the same chemicals, I cannot. Would you consider alternative treatment? Please check out Urban Greenery or BeeSafe.

    Brenda

Dear Brenda,

I do extensive reading before choosing products to put on my lawn. I want to protect my family. Reactions to the product we use are very rare. I am sorry you are so rare. Maybe I can send you a short list and next year you can help pick something that does not harm you.

    Dr. Xian Ling (Julie)
    she / her / hers
    Senior Bioscience Consultant
    PharmaLogic

Dear Julie,

It doesn't take a scientist to know that our planet and our people are in peril. Why you are opposed to keeping your dandelions, or at least removing them by hand, I don't know. It's the best solution for everyone involved and for the world beyond your 0.3 acre plot.

    Brenda

Dear Brenda,
What does your husband do? Aside from put up with you?

Dr. Xian Ling (Julie)
she / her / hers
Senior Bioscience Consultant
PharmaLogic

Julie,
I don't have a husband. My partner, Kelly, is currently spending time with her parents in Calgary. Her brother died of cancer last month.
Brenda
(as in Brenda K. Lunney, Naturopathic Doctor)

Dear Dr. Lunney,
My deepest sympathies for the loss of your brother-in-law. This must be a terrible time. I have no wish to make things more stressful. Also, I am sorry I judged some things about you and your partner.
- J

Dear Brenda,
Thank you again for mowing last week. Ella is thrilled. She is wearing a bee-proof suit and earning 50 cents for every dandelion she removes from the lawn with tools.
- J

Dear Brenda,
Again, I am sorry and also sorry we fought over email. I noticed the For Sale sign on your lawn, and more mowing but not by you. I hope everything is ok.
- J

Dear Brenda,

Are you checking this email even if you have moved away? I do apologize and would like to know if you received my apology.

  - J

Dear Brenda,

It would be nice if you could at least send a short reply to acknowledge my apology. I feed badly and want to know you got it.

  - J

Dear Brenda,

It is making me a little bit crazy to not know if you received my apology. Please reply even just with the word received or something. We don't have to say more.

  - J

Dear Brenda,

In case you are still checking this email, I wanted to tell you that Ella earned $23 removing dandelions. She is becoming expensive haha! But I don't mind at all. She enjoys this so much she went to your old lawn and removed some there too although I told her it is not our business. This has been something I never learned before, how to work with neighbours around property and things together. I hope you know that I am sorry. Please acknowledge my email when you can. Thank you,

  - Julie

Dear Brenda,

Did you ever talk to others much in our neighbourhood? Ella plays with Josef at number 4 but the parents don't do much except work out play dates. We don't hang out together. You were the only person here I talked to if you count this as talking to someone. My husband did not want to come to Canada. He chose to stay in China so I came alone with Ella. It has been hard to meet people.

  - J

Dear Brenda,

I have to stop emailing you, I know. It still bothers me that you never replied to my apology. I wish you well. Hopefully somewhere you forgive me and wish me well too. Ella said it was nice that we learned to care more about bees because they can do such good things for everyone even though they can hurt her. Thank you,

  - J

Dear Dr. Ling,

My name is Kelly Tolman. I used to be Brenda Lunney's partner. You moved in shortly before I left to be with my family in Calgary during the last stages of my brother's illness.

I'm writing because this email has indeed been active, but with a different kind of activity. It turns out Brenda was seeing someone (several someones, truth be told) while I was away, and even before that. Brenda left quite suddenly and didn't change her passwords on anything. She took advantage of my trust this way, terribly. She knew I was never one to look at her email and texts. Maybe I'm a masochist but I'm going through it all now, trying to piece together this other life she had during this last year of our relationship when I wasn't around much. Apparently you were a part of it in some way.

I know what it's like to try to rebuild a life and have so little terra firma from which to start. I don't know if she would apologize to you or forgive you, but I do. Your little girl sounds adorable, and I hope you appreciate the joy of one another no matter who comes and goes in your lives.

I am shutting this email account down now. Be well,

  K.

Rolfie

During the heat wave of my twenty-fourth year, my friend Raulphina lay for five days on her bed, wearing the same barely-nothing clothing, the floor model fan blasting ineffectually.

"She's not even checking social media," said her mother over the land line.

I hung up and drove to the house over scorching side streets. Her mother greeted me at the door, wearing the same sheen that covered us all. "How are you faring?" she asked.

I could never calculate Raulphina. Why did you ever name her that.

"Fine," I said. Then I realized I should smile, so I did. Her mother smiled back.

Down the hall in her room, Rolfie was 100 percent as described over the phone. Splayed, silent, breathing, absorbed by the punishing heat and her allied detachment. I pushed my bottom teeth out beneath my upper lip. This was unconscious. Upon realizing what I was doing, I repeated and exaggerated, hoping it would make her laugh. It didn't.

I sat. I talked to Rolfie, but really to myself. I said things about our friends, about TikTok, Netflix. I didn't expect a response. I wasn't disappointed.

After a while, the skies darkened somewhat. Thunder sounded off the ocean, muted but close. A watchful dog. The air changed not at all.

Rolfie. The name we gave her out of kindness, out of hope for a new identity. No one in her family could tell how far the name Raulphina went back in generations, or even what relation that person had been. The name was remarkable, my friend not so much. "Raulphie," I giggled one night, years ago, at a sleepover. "Or how about Rolf? Like Wolf, with an 'R.' Something wild, something mysterious. You could be anything—an actor, a runway model, a jet-setting crazy famous influencer, come on!"

Rolf seemed pleased but unsure. We moved on to eating too many chips, watching too many horror movies, and sleeping poorly in her parents' basement.

In the year that followed, Rolf added an "i" and an "e" and continued to seem pleased but unsure. In physical appearance, she adopted the persona of Wednesday Addams meets Anne of Green Gables. Her character developed the interesting qualities of neither.

"You're such a good friend," came her mother's loud whisper from the doorway, easily heard over the huffing and ticking of the fan. I turned in acknowledgement. Her mother's understated nod before she continued down the hall added, "You've done so well."

My meticulous smile required greater effort this time.

Have I? I thought.

She means, yes, you have, given ....

... given that both of your parents overdosed when you were a toddler and you were raised by your grandparents, who were nice but always old, who had no clue how to teach a girl to navigate a world fifty years younger, who had no clue that you could have taken them to the cleaners for their money or their mental health. Or both. They had no idea that any of this had even crossed your mind.

I supposed I had turned out half decent.

My grandparents told me of my origins just after I turned fourteen. They told me by the time the town wanted to but before it did. I was a mess initially, but I was one of those people who "did well in therapy." The way I saw everything, and everyone, changed—my grandparents, my friends, my home, myself. Then it changed again, and again. It still changes, the knowledge painful by times, freeing by others; sometimes it's a disorienting kaleidoscope of both.

No one else ever saw me differently. They had always known.

Here, today, Rolfie didn't see me at all.

"Is it because you don't want to? Or you can't?" I asked.

I sat with my strange chosen-family sister awhile longer. The fan oscillated and oscillated, on and on. Rolfie's pale, billowy shirt and shorts leapt in a different way each time. Her long, black, horizontal pigtails didn't move at all. I had left my phone in the car on purpose but was beginning to feel the blood itch of tech separation.

"I named you, remember?" I murmured. "I don't even know who named me."

I looked to the floor for a time.

"But I turned out okay. So they say."

The thunder never progressed beyond a warning. The heavy heat never moved at all.

I rose and waved at Rolfie. "Text me later," I said, smiling at the likely absurdity of my words more than at her. "A bunch of us are going out."

tic. tic. tic. tic. tic. the fan.

"Are you sure you're not doing this on purpose?"

tic. tic. tic. tic. tic.

"See ya."

I sat in the industrial oven of my car, breathing, the air leaving my lungs cooler than it entered. It would be a decision to turn the key. It would be a decision to put my foot on the brake, to put the car in reverse. To leave the driveway, to return to my grandparents' house, to go to work, to sleep with a stranger, to name another friend.

Rolfie's mother came out, worried that something was wrong. I gave another big smile, snatched my phone, and held it up. Look how responsible I am, checking my texts before driving, this said. Then I dropped the phone on the passenger seat, startled and agitated, as though caught naked or stealing. The tires chirped as I sped away.

Look how well I turned out.

Critical

Aquatica: A Regrettable Dive into Murky Waters

Review by D'Arcy Sinclair

How could we not just vibrate in anticipation of the opening of Dwyer Bay's latest culinary adventure: a dockside seafood restaurant finally open year-round, with décor that completely and alarmingly escapes tragedy, and a wine list that wasn't constructed by the middle-aged dregs of the college football alumni?

The menu was released online the night before opening. There were lineups. There was a VIP list. On these accounts, I declined the opening night invitation sent from the personal email of Chef Laurel himself.

One week into service, my seating finally came. While I had heard positively of Laurel's work in other parts of North America, I had yet to experience it myself. Why he had chosen to set up shop in Dwyer Bay was a bit of a mystery to me. Is this the type of town where we see the stars only as they explode into orbit on their way up, and as they re-enter in a piteous ball of flames on their way down? The details would speak to me.

My senses were tingling in foretaste. So were my tastebuds from the opener of champagne and Dwyer Bay oysters, shucked and served directly at my table by a young waitress whose bloodline must hail from endless generations of Swedish royalty. For the oysters: no mignonette, no variation of a cocktail sauce. Was this deliberate or suspect? Time would tell. It is true that Dwyer Bay's very own oysters stand tall on their sweet, robust merit. The rest of the world is blessed by their mere existence.

Since oysters constitute a fifth food group for me, another appetizer had to be sampled. I chose the tuna tartare with maple Dijon and scooped parmesan served on a multi-seed cracker. The cracker itself is a creation of Laurel's home kitchen, and now available for messy cracker consumption in the comfort of your own home, should you choose to pick up a package at Jody D's Organic Market at sixteen dollars a bag. At sixteen dollars a bag, these crackers should be life changing. They're not.

Neither was this appetizer. It screamed for a port reduction with the Dijon instead of maple syrup. I'm always up for a wildly mismatched Clash-of-the-Condiments, but only if there emerges a winner. The local maple contender was a saccharine yet gloomy spectre, blinded by the light as it emerged from its dingy dwelling of Saint Malachi's basement, where its sole job to date has been, with mixed results, to enliven the annual pancake breakfast. When unleashed in the same arena as the bitter *aristo-cratie* of the Dijon, it did nothing but trade insults and punches, and wound up riding in the same ambulance. Poor, poor tuna tartare. At least it was cooked properly.

A simple crab bisque always turns my head faster than Priscilla Presley on a Tuesday night re-run of The Naked Gun Part 2½. Oh, and what yoga pose is this? Laurel had chosen to arrange the claws in the form of the Tadasana pose sticking out of the soup. Why?? This made the soup completely inaccessible by spoon without sending the claw splashing down into the soup more inappositely than a drunk model spilling off a runway (and God knows we all love a drunk model spilling off a runway). The garlic scapes added to the scene, but only by way of making the posing crab look like a Medusa crab, which is in no world necessary. Beyond the utter fail of a presentation, I still clung to a faint hope for blissful bisque. It wasn't the worst, although I wasn't sure of all the flavours I was experiencing, especially the lingering bitter one.

Prior to serving the main course, the Swedish Vision returned with a mini wine menu offering a selection of pairings. They were contingent on my choice of side dish to accompany the "Swordfish Canvas," whatever wonderful surprise that was to be. Her return was more glorious than her initial appearance. I think there might have been a costume change. The custom pairing menu was actually a good idea. But, like all good ideas, it cannot exist in isolation. I was unable to recall my wine selection once the Canvas was paraded out and placed in front of me as though it was the Christ child himself.

The swordfish steak was as pale as the buttocks of an elderly woman drained of disease by leeches. Across the steak, written in squid ink, was a skillful yet misguided use of the Modern Love font: BLESS.

Another Canvas was being delivered to a nearby table. I stopped the server en route. "What does theirs say?" I asked, wide-eyed with wonder and fear. He lowered the plate. DREAM, said the Canvas.

Still stunned with disbelief, I began to poke at the side dish, which was called "Treasures of the Sea." I had been expecting caviar and roe and the like. Said items were present within a translucent tube that I finally recognized as the digestive casing of a lobster. The accompanying salad was shredded kale with fennel seeds and truffle oil. All I could focus on at this point was the intestinal endgame of a lobster's innards, which, like the earlier *kaffeeklatsch* of Medusa crab and garlic scapes, had zero business on the real estate of my plate.

By this time, I was utterly exhausted with disappointment at the endless display of poor culinary choices, yet morbidly curious about the dessert options. These did not arrive on the sultry lips of the roving Swedish artwork, but rather on the smile of the male server who had showed me his swordfish earlier. He presented me with options such as blue marlin meringue, salmon mousse with white chocolate drizzle, and beet sorbet. Despite the latter being the only reasonable dessert, which seemed completely out of place among the others, I went with—nay, needed—a large vodka martini. They almost nailed it.

Anyone who reads my work or follows me on socials knows that I love a culinary adventure. In fact, this is my *raison d'être*. But when someone promises you such an adventure and leaves you feeling sorrowful, confused, and nearly $200 poorer, you must become an advocate for your fellow gastronomes. Consider my voice yours. Take the plunge into your own creativity and concoct a seafood soirée in the clear waters of your own home, where the only colons in attendance will remain intact and where they belong—unseen, within the glorious presence of yourself and your fine friends.

Once he finished reading the piece, the editor of The Chronicle slowly lowered the tablet to his desk. He folded his arms on top and buried his face in them.

"What?" asked D'Arcy.

Charles raised his head, the red of his face dissonant with that of his hair. "You'll destroy it. Dwyer Bay—YOUR hometown—finally gets a restaurant worthy of review by its own world-famous critic, and you DESTROY it." He took a deep breath and looked out the window, speaking to no one in particular. "How do I even run this?"

D'Arcy sat, his silence an illusion of sympathetic listening.

"Sausage is cased in intestine," imparted Charles.

"The seeds of one's progeny should not be stuffed into one's own intestines, even if one is a bottom-feeding creature of the sea."

"I somehow doubt anyone but you would care about that detail."

"Well, detail is my job, for which you hired me."

Charles raised his eyebrows and exhaled slowly. "I have to run this." He continued his habitual process of talking-to-himself-with-others-present. "The whole town is expecting it. The whole province is expecting it. All of your people are expecting it. I can't not run it. By the same token, I can't endorse the destruction of the first good thing to happen here in years. This restaurant employs like twenty-five people. That'll double in summer. Corporate conventions are booked around it for an entire year in advance. Dwyer Bay's own celebrity can't ruin its economic resurgence."

"Did you like the line about the server showing me his swordfish?"

Charles stared at the wall behind D'Arcy. Finally, he shook his head, and rose in conclusion of the meeting. "You've put me in an impossible position," he said.

"You'll do the right thing."

"And what exactly is the right thing, in your mind?"

"Our little hillbilly fishing village doesn't need the wool pulled over its eyes by a has-been chef looking for cheap real estate and praying for a final shot at the Food Network. We deserve better, and that is the truthful motivation of my review."

"Right isn't always best," called Charles as D'Arcy was partway down the hall.

"You're wrong," shot D'Arcy without turning.

Still soaring on the righteous deed of his article, D'Arcy decided to pop into a downtown café for a late breakfast and some internet time. It was impossible for him to do anything incognito in most places, especially here, especially this past week. His trademark massive red square glasses and dark grey hair with its wide, white bands along the top and sides weren't dumbed down for the occasion either. People had been mostly respectful of his space. A few café patrons failed at discretion by taking selfies over their shoulders. One approached for an autograph, and graciously left once the napkin was signed. Once the initial buzz died down, D'Arcy began sifting through emails on his phone. He realized he was starving only when the server arrived at his table with her notepad and a well-loved stub of a pencil.

"Not here to review us too, I hope," she said. D'Arcy looked up to her smile of crooked teeth and unusually plump lips, homely yet luminous. He instantly liked her. He would never hire her as a server, of course. But he liked her.

"No, my dear, no no." He shook his head and waved off the idea. "One just wants to eat sometimes, wouldn't you say? It is a basic need, after all." She nodded and waited as he revisited the menu, then shut it, undecided. "Your favourite sandwich. And an allongé. The sandwich must have meat in it, though."

She nodded and scribed. "Are you with us long?"

"Only until the review is published later this afternoon."

"Did you like it at the new place?"

He tilted his head and pursed his lips. "A gentleman doesn't eat and tell. At least not before he is published."

She smiled again and headed for the kitchen. He felt himself melting a little in her presence and wasn't sure why. It wasn't her hair, or her build, or her face, or her well-picked consignment attire. It must have been the smile. After all, he wasn't entirely gay.

The sandwich was good. Better than his emails, at least, which he found particularly tedious. A book tour was coming up. Ronan, his latest par-amour and assistant, had many questions about hotels in places D'Arcy had not yet stayed. While mildly annoyed at this process, D'Arcy, like Ronan, felt the weight of accurate decisions on their layered relationship.

D'Arcy moved on to his daily Google of himself. This always lifted his spirits, even when the feed was relatively quiet, as it tended to be immedi-ately prior to a new review. He was satisfied by the animated countdown timer and one-liner in Toronto's *Tucker*: *D'Arcy Sinclair's Latest Shock-sational Restaurant Review in T-minus ...*

What might I do, what might I do, thought D'Arcy, tapping his phone against his lips and staring out the window at the intermittent mid-afternoon foot and road traffic of the petite sea-side town. His adult life had carried him away early, into circles of "friends" far different from the tiny circle he had chosen to cut ties with here. He no longer had any family in the area to speak of. His parents had neither understood him nor tried to. They had, however, kept a binder of clippings of all his pub-lished work. Once they learned to use a computer, they printed his online reviews, including all the comments, and arranged them with great care in the binder. He found this when he and his sister were sorting through the contents of the family home prior to its sale. "You'd never know you hadn't been here in ten years," she said, the sarcasm unintended, yet fully felt by both.

Not going there, thought D'Arcy as he rose to pay. His generous tip elicited a final smile, which he knew he would have gotten anyway. This brightened his mood. He decided on a prolonged stroll through town back to the hotel. He texted the driver he had at his disposal to say he would be in touch later regarding airport transportation.

The overcast late spring afternoon made for a disorienting transition from the brightly lit hallway into the dark hotel room. The square of the singular window was minimally brighter. D'Arcy picked a book from his luggage and cringed at the dusty rose plush chair prior to lowering himself into it.

He barely reached the seat before bolting up again, agitated. The book sailed across the room, bouncing off his suitcase and landing face down on the bed. D'Arcy stood at the window. He closed his eyes and inhaled deeply, as his therapist had taught him. He exhaled slowly, as his therapist had taught him. He opened his eyes to find the pier below unchanged in its grey and brown tones from thirty years ago, when he had last looked down on it from other rooms within the hotel. The obsolescent marine gas pumps were somehow no more corroded.

In this moment, one block away, there was a shiny new restaurant coated in all forms of ridiculous hype, undoubtedly the product of a regional economic development program that funded a bonanza of unoriginal thoughts and liquid lunches. D'Arcy felt rattled. The intersection of his past and current lives was unbearable. "Why did I agree to come back here?" he asked himself in a whisper.

There was never anything for me here ...

Wait. The money.

D'Arcy snuffled out of his nose. He had come back for a contract.

A contract. Business. Money.

Like the money they all paid me in this room, the other rooms. More than once they paid me ...

Not staying here, he thought. He threw his remaining items into his suitcase, zipped it up, and sent it flying on its wheels toward the door. He grabbed his coat and his phone and managed a harried pause to check his teeth in the mirror. He descended to the lobby.

The hotel bar greeted him with a couple of free drinks, which were no better or worse than the martini from the unjustly gilded restaurant nouveau. He was further greeted with attention and flattery from the patrons who chose to approach him. He received them with his headliner smile, grand gestures, and colourful accounts of his travels. He began to breathe normally. He was D'Arcy Sinclair. What a triumphant way to conclude this abysmal trip, spending time among the locals, just as *The Chronicle* arrives! A rain-soaked delivery driver dropped a brick of papers onto the bar. The bartender and patrons descended on it.

"Enjoy the read!" D'Arcy flourished as he exited.

On his way toward the main doors, he stopped at a rickety box display containing magazines, pamphlets for local attractions, and the freshly placed *Chronicle*. He snapped up a copy, curious as to what sort of layout Charles would have chosen for the piece.

Aquatica Dives into Uncharted Waters

Review by Darcy St-Clair

How could we not just vibrate in anticipation of the opening of Dwyer Bay's latest culinary adventure, a dockside seafood restaurant finally open year-round, with décor that completely and alarmingly escapes tragedy and a wine list constructed with international flair?

The menu was released online the night before opening. The hits kept on coming to the website. There were lineups. There was a VIP list. I declined the opening night invitation, allowing some time for the kinks to be worked out prior to my seaside hometown visit.

So my seating finally comes, one week into service. While I have heard positively of Chef Laurel's work in other parts of North America, I had yet to experience it myself. Would Dwyer Bay be the next link in the unbroken chain of his successes? The details would speak to me. My senses were tingling, starting with my tastebuds, from the opener of champagne and Dwyer Bay oysters. These were shucked and served directly at my table by a fabulous young waitress whose shucking finesse was beyond her years. No mignonette, no variation of a cocktail sauce; it is true that our Dwyer Bay oysters are seafaring ambassadors the world over.

Since oysters constitute a fifth food group for me, another appetizer had to be sampled. I chose the tuna tartare with maple Dijon and scooped parmesan served on a multi-seed cracker. The cracker is a creation of Laurel's home kitchen, and now available at Jody D's Organic Market, should you wish to enjoy such a delight in your own home. The maple Dijon turned out to be a Clash-of-the-Condiments Title Fight between the hometown favourite, a local maple syrup evoking sweet memories of our annual Saint Malachi's family breakfast fundraiser, and the spicy European mustard rival. The tuna tartare was prepared perfectly.

A simple crab bisque always turns my head like the fresh yet classic beauty of Meghan Markle. Out of the soup rose the crab claws in the form of the Tadasana yoga pose. Seafood of tranquility! The pose serves to draw the diner's gaze further into the flow of the piece, augmented by garlic scapes. The flavour was slightly bitter and lingering on the palate.

Then it was time for main course. Prior to this, my most excellent server returned with a mini wine menu offering a selection of pairings that were contingent on the side dish I would choose to accompany the "Swordfish Canvas," whatever delight that was to be. What a fabulous idea, this custom wine pairing! I completely forgot what I chose for wine as the Canvas was paraded out and placed before me.

The swordfish steak was perfectly pale with a delicate silk finish. Across it was written, in the aptly chosen Modern Love font bequeathed of squid ink: BLESS.

Another Canvas was being delivered to a nearby table, and I was compelled to stop the server en route. "What does theirs say?" I asked, breathless with curiosity. He lowered the plate. DREAM, replied the Canvas.

Returning to the delights of my own plate, I began to acquaint myself with the side dish, which was called "Treasures of the Sea." I had been expecting caviar and roe and the like. These were indeed present, within a translucent casing skillfully extracted from the lobster. The accompanying salad was a shredded kale with fennel seed and truffle oil. What a divine mix of colour and texture!

By this time, I was overwhelmed by the endless display of culinary creativity, yet still inquisitive about the dessert options. These arrived via the courtly male server who had delivered the swordfish earlier. He presented options such as blue marlin meringue, salmon mousse with white chocolate drizzle, and a beet sorbet. The latter seemed out of place in theme, although a palate-cleansing option is always a good choice at this point in a meal. In my case, I was ready for a classic palate cleansing à la dry martini. They nailed it.

Anyone who reads my work or follows me on socials knows that I love a culinary adventure—in fact, I live for it. But when someone delivers on such an adventure, you must become an advocate. Consider my voice yours, and feel inspired to visit Aquatica; or pick up some multi-seed crackers and a variety of seafood delights, and dare to create a seafood soirée for your friends in the comfort of your very own home ... though I doubt your experience could ever rival that of Aquatica.

As the last truck left the loading dock and the internet files began to populate, Charles meandered through the building. He chatted with his two staff reporters and administrative assistant about nothing in particular. Back in his office, he opened a bottle of whisky that he kept in his desk drawer for stressful situations or emergencies, which were often one and the same. He sank the first pour and reclined in his chair and sipped the second. The last draw cleared his mouth as he set the glass and bottle back in the drawer, clinking in perfect time with the roaring and stomping that increased in volume as the distance shortened between himself and the full force of D'Arcy Sinclair on his way up the corridor.

The office door blew open and bounced off the wall. D'Arcy took advantage of its return momentum and smashed it shut. The doorframe and wall were still vibrating as D'Arcy, the red of his face at one with the frames of his glasses, screamed, "WHAT HAVE YOU DONE!!?"

"Care to sit?" asked Charles, extending a hand toward a chair.

"This isn't my work!" D'Arcy hollered. "You can't publish something that isn't my work! In fact, it's a terrible bastardization of my work! You threw the intent of the review altogether, you removed most of the signature phrasing, and you published it under my name—which wasn't even my name, by the way, but you knew that!"

"That is your name as it is written under your high school graduation photo on the wall down by the gym."

D'Arcy didn't allow this to land. "You're printing a correction tomorrow."

"We will print a correction of the name. Or, rather, a mis-correction of the name."

"You will print a correction of the whole damn thing. Or you'll be sued."

"Did you re-post the review on all your social media yet?"

"How could I??" D'Arcy threw his hands up in the air in exasperation. "The confusion! You are going to print the correction, in full, and I am going to get my online settled. I can't believe I agreed to exclusive first publishing with you. In PRINT," he hissed. "Hometown concession. Amateur hour on my part. And Meghan Markle? Really??"

"I'm not doing a reprint," said Charles.

"No, no, no, no." D'Arcy shook his head to punctuate each word. "You have to. You're done, otherwise. You'll be sunk. This whole paper will be sunk."

"No," said Charles, steady.

D'Arcy laughed. It was a strange and sad sound. "What in the hell makes you think you are going to get away with this?"

"You," replied Charles.

D'Arcy opened his mouth to tear another strip off Charles, but instead closed it and snickered.

"If you publish the original now," continued Charles, "you will look like an ass. Mind you, you've made an entire career of being an ass. An eloquent one. But still. There is nothing eloquent about how this would roll out. The 'integrity' on which you pride yourself for culinary excellence and your scathing style—"

"Shock-sational. My style is shock-sational."

"—in some demented service of authenticity would fall completely flat. Not remotely congruent with your work or image. It would look confusing and unprofessional. Especially since you did indeed agree to exclusive first publishing with us." Charles leaned forward in his chair, opened the drawer, and placed the bottle of whisky back on the desk. "Drink?" he asked, looking up. D'Arcy scowled and headed for the door. "No?" replied Charles to himself.

"You've put me in an impossible position," said D'Arcy, his hand on the doorknob.

Charles refilled his glass and leaned back in his chair. He didn't bother raising his head as he dismissed the celebrity. "It really wasn't your best work anyway."

D'Arcy hauled the door shut behind him, making the initial slam seem a caress. Agitated and unable to wait, he bypassed the elevator and cascaded down four flights of stairs. He sent the exit door flying by its crash bar, crossed the lobby in a shot, and launched himself into the backseat of the waiting car. "Airport!" he barked. The car pulled away while D'Arcy dialed Ronan and put his phone to his ear, seething. "Talk me through this nightmare before I do something everyone involved here will regret."

The heated call continued at the gate drop-off. Still on his phone, D'Arcy leapt from the car, opened the trunk, grabbed his suitcase, and ripped into the terminal. Ensuring that his passenger was fully inside the building, the driver sat for a moment. He reached into his jacket pocket for his own phone and dialed his wife to tell her that he was on his way home. As he ended the call, he realized that he hadn't said a single word aloud for the entirety of his week as D'Arcy Sinclair's driver.

He smiled to himself as he folded the newspaper on the passenger seat, ready to deliver it to his wife as she had asked. He put the car in gear and drove away. At least the asshole had managed to write a half-decent review.

The Dream Estate

Saturday morning on the thirty-ninth floor of the Saunders Building, a driven panel of investors and economists were working. They did not want to be working on a weekend, yet they were. They were highly accomplished in their careers. They left behind dogs, spouses, children, early morning runs, prolonged slumber, markets, errands, and coffee with their lovers.

Karina was one of them, yet she was not one of them at all.

She didn't leave behind anything like boyfriends or girlfriends, early morning workouts, or overpriced brunches. She didn't leave anything behind. Her dreams followed her from her bed into every waking day, interlacing themselves in and around the hours until she went to sleep again. Their vivid sublimeness, devastation, or measures of both formed an intimate apparel unseen by others over her skin, her eyes, her heart. The colours and textures were bizarre and shocking. They were not conducive to habituation, and therefore to forgetting.

The voice—was it coming from the barista working the lobby coffee bar, or from the young woman who tried to serve her the fish omelette with all three of her hands sometime during the night? Their facial features were so similar.

The dreams that accompanied Karina to the thirty-ninth floor on this Saturday morning disentangled themselves from her shoulders and floated across the boardroom. They collected as though on a giant screen and began a transition wipe from ceiling to floor, dissolving the 1970s faux wood panelling enough for her to see the modern, exposed concrete walls behind her colleagues' heads across the table.

"Hutch and Dutchess is climbing. It is worth moving the funds there now," she said on cue, her face a light purple hue from her laptop screen. The screen was reflected in her large glasses, which reflected smaller purple versions of the screen, then herself, then itself, then herself.

Itself herself itself herself, said radio voice, a woman's.

"I accept this," said Anna. Garnet nodded beside her.

"Finally," said Karina, without attempt to disguise her disdain.

"Tyreese?" asked Anna, looking to the employee in the chair to Karina's left.

The grey and navy yoga bolsters lay in piles, dozens of them. Sometimes they moved. An instructor spoke imperceptibly. Someone tapped at the door over and over, ignored by the instructor. The insides of Karina's chest felt orange. She knew, as always, that no one else saw any of this. She sometimes wondered what they saw. Was it as bland as Anna's personality, Garnet's attire? Was that somehow comforting?

There was a short pause as Bolsher projected a series of financials on the smartboard. The team looked from the big screen to their personal ones. Karina saw the numbers crawling about on the big screen, slowly pushing those from other lines, horizontally or vertically. She recalled a dream from back when she was in high school. Its memory had long stayed with her, most often as a cellular impression of molecules morphing into numbers morphing into molecules, jockeying for place in her organs.

The meeting continued in a clockwise sequence of contributions from around the table. Karina brought up her next research document. The Duke of Edinburgh shone in a life-sized, translucent two-dimensional image beside her. Smiling, he bobbed from side to side like a character ready for play in a video game. She ignored him. The image abruptly swiped up. Under the table, cards were shuffled and the voice asked if we were ready for the red pills. The voices bothered her the most.

Karina shifted her attention to the hairline hum of the building's HVAC system. Outside the many windows high above the city, the wind pushed vast sheets of low clouds in a rapid, coated sequence beneath the sun, creating a strobe effect of the light's intensity. Through the clouds, she heard her name.

"That tech is done, according to my trends." She took a sip of her coffee and prepared for an argument from Bolsher. He paused as he thought about giving her one, then changed his mind. As much as they all found her a bit odd, they knew her to be stunningly accurate in her figures and research.

Beyond Bolsher, the geese moved in and out of the AstroTurf. Their beaks wove themselves a bright green plastic basket between the broken white yard lines in a stadium that was microscopic and colossal all at once, all to the white noise soundtrack of HVAC.

Open the cottage, open the cottage, open the cottage. The family opened the cottage.

"We'll need the actual figures on that one."

"I figured, sending now."

Jordan smiled from across the table, acknowledging the pun Karina had no intention of making. She recognized it after the fact. Feeling shy, she made herself smile back. How would he ever understand? The giant white letter G, three stories tall, crept down the dark, empty street, leaving a trail of milk behind it, around him.

As they collectively scrolled on their laptops to page ninety-four, the employees were distracted by their phones all receiving an emergency notification at once. Karina felt her insides invaded from the left as the woman, the young nurse with the black bangs, got too close in her personal space. "You'll have to take her home and care for her," she said, pointing with her long arm toward Chris. The arm expanded three feet, four feet, five feet to where Chris lay writhing on a hospital bed in an open ward, a full-body mass of red blisters. The smell of iron and puss turned everyone's clothing a mustard green. "The skin graft is complete."

Karina despised Chris. Her stomach dove in helplessness. "I can't," she whispered in place of a scream.

No one heard her. Phones blazed and buzzed. People made sounds of curiosity, disbelief, fear, deliberate control. Karina heard the confining buzz of doors locking electronically. The collective stomach of the room dove in helplessness, and the room itself came alarmingly into focus.

Karina saw the red banner splashed across her phone, the chaotic panorama of coworkers grabbing their computers, books, phones, drinks, glasses, and sweaters, and shoving them under the table before ducking under it themselves.

ALERT ALERT ALERT SHELTER IN PLACE, said the banner. EARTHQUAKE IN CITY CENTRE

Earthquake in city centre, somewhere far beneath the thirty-nine floors below.

Karina dropped under the table and braced up against one of its legs. People were texting madly. The power went off. The darkened room accentuated the light from phone screens and terror under the table. Karina watched the terror. It was pale blue. It made jagged figure eights of her colleagues' hearts and lungs. The floor under everyone's knees and legs began to bounce.

The buzzing of the bees intensified. The combs were stacking and stacking around Karina, up to her neck, keeping her warm. "Bring that over," said the old, bearded beekeeper. Karina willed the voice and its phrase into repeat.

bring that over bring that over bring that over bring that over

She held the presence of the bees and the man close for as long as they would let her, while an indeterminate amount of time passed.

Stillness. The lights came back on. The building's mechanics revved into action. Colleagues sighed, laughed, cried, shook, called loved ones. They crawled out from under the table. The diaspora of dandelion seeds on the wind, it was a hot slow day on the plains. Where were they going now.

Karina nodded in acknowledgement of the event. She was fine, she replied when asked. She packed up her computer, her lunch container, her purse. They received the all-clear and began, for the first and only time, to descend the dizzying thirty-nine flights of stairs on foot at varying speeds. Karina's was slower. Each floor of the concrete stairwell smelled different, like each floor of her apartment building, like dorm rooms in residence, like each day-box on the calendar the summer her grandmother died.

She moved through the rest of her Saturday filtering images waking and dreamt, wishing the beekeeper to reappear among them.

Reconstructionism

The forensic unit had begun its work prior to Inspector Jason Cameron's arrival. Jason's phone vibrated in his pocket as he was concluding a press conference. The familiar dot-dash-dot pattern indicated something unfortunate. Meanwhile, his spirits were lifted by the prospect of saying, "This concludes the press conference. Lillian Stapleton will field any questions you may have. Thank you."

Jason ripped through town and the S-curve-heavy road to the ocean front park, one of many that provided excellent tourism dollars in summer. It was now late October. The incident was not likely tourist related.

The constable at the park entrance greeted him with a nod, inclining his head toward the wood-lined path that led to the water.

He could hear the team down on the beach, their voices volleying measurements and observations. He was alone when he reached the clearing, a picnic area on the waterfront. It was nearing sunset on an overcast day. Grey touched grey along a gentle horizon. A row of inverted picnic tables had been hauled to the tree line and chained together for the winter, leaving a lone bench at the edge of the bank.

Jason stopped at the bench. It was unexpectedly and invitingly decorated. A delicate fabric was draped over the length of the seat, alternating purple and pink. It fluttered intermittently at one end while a large wicker basket held down the other. The basket was well used and well-tended. Bits of leather shoelace had been woven into places of wear.

The bench's adornments were deliberate and human against the open sky and water, the ocean's October sound brittle along the rocky shore. Jason was absorbed by the setup.

A head popped up over the edge of the bank. "Jay!" the officer called. It was Corporal Neil Logan, who happened to be Jason's best friend.

Jason covered his surprise with a cough. "Photog done yet?" he called back.

"Just about."

Jason inched around the bench as if around a remarkable sand sculpture. The contents of the basket appeared in view. A little book of poetry, indie press. A newspaper folded with a partially completed sudoku. Organic crackers. A travel container of cut vegetables, about half full. A bottle of champagne, three-quarters empty. Two glasses, one clean.

"She was on a date," said Logan.

"Was she?" asked Jason. He bent to look more closely at the glasses. "Not sure. Who found her?"

Logan turned to indicate the forensic identification photographer in the water. "Sarah, oddly enough. She was trying to have a day off."

Jason cleared his throat, stifling a laugh. He had to work continuously at reminding himself that he was Logan's superior. "No way. That's brutal." Jason looked up and down the beach, his gaze landing where Sarah's day off had her suited up and hip-deep in the water, though it had begun with the intention of photographing something other than deviance and death. She lowered the camera to verify a shot on the screen, then stood straight and waved it in the air.

"Clear!"

The officers and coroner's assistants on shore moved forward in a wave of their own, breeching the cold to retrieve the body. Jason dropped down the shallow bank.

"Mid-fifties, I'd say," huffed Logan as he assisted in turning the body over on shore. "Head wound at the right posterior of the skull. Puncture. Recent."

"Mmmm," muttered Jason, looking down at the body. The hair was long, white, and darker at the ends, an heirloom of younger years. Maybe her face had been attractive. It was hard to tell. She wore hippy-like clothes: wide-legged pants in a canvas fabric, a poncho, a knitted scarf that had mostly unwrapped itself from her neck.

Along with the scarf, a small purse had somehow remained with the body. Logan nodded to a tech, who pried open the sodden red faux leather and dug through bank and loyalty cards. The tech pulled out a driver's licence and handed it to Logan. "Marie Hinckey," he read. "Age … fifty-eight? Botten Road." He handed the licence to Jason.

The ultimate contrast between a picture taken while a victim was alive and the image of their corpse always fascinated Jason. Marie clearly had not wanted her licence picture taken. Eyes: green. "Motorcycle classification, bus classification," observed Jason aloud. He handed the license to another tech. "Come back to us with the family info." The tech nodded and left the beach.

"Let's go," Jason said to Logan, leaving the coroner's team with the body.

"Where do we start?" asked Logan.

Jason stopped and looked up and down the beach. "Not sure. This doesn't smell of homicide to me," he said.

"Two wine glasses," said Logan, liking his theory.

"One looked pretty clean … and there's not enough food there for two. Plus, the sudoku. Does that spell 'hot date' to you?"

Logan laughed. "Fair point. Two glasses, though?"

"Hmmm. In memory of someone? Or maybe wishful thinking, putting it out there to the universe? Maybe both?"

"This so doesn't sound like you."

"I'm not thinking 'like' me. I'm aiming to think 'like' her."

They climbed the drop and found themselves back at the bench. Logan began to push the contents of the basket around with a pen, searching for support of either theory. Jason took another deliberate look up and down the shoreline. His eyes landed on some deadfall. It appeared new, the yellow of the trunks vibrant. "That storm last week," he said.

"Yeah."

"They've laid off the staff here for the season, right? No one checking in after high winds?"

"Correct."

Jason stood, envisioning the moment. "See that last tree—the one angled strangely to the others—check that one for blood. I'm wondering if she was a bit buzzed. Maybe she tripped, or maybe she leaned on the stack and destabilized something accidentally. Then maybe she staggered a few steps and passed out, tide took her before she could fully handle consciousness." He paused. "There must have been no one around here all day but her. I hope she just let go. Sailed away."

Logan looked at his best friend and superior officer. "That's quite the narrative, Jay-bud."

"Well." Jason checked his phone and zipped his anorak higher. "Wouldn't you want to go peacefully?"

Logan laughed. "I wanna go in my sleep, or because my parachute didn't open, one or the other. Anyway, sure. I'll go get the techs on the tree." He headed back toward the cliff. "You outta here, Sir?"

"*Sir*," scoffed Jason. "Only in front of other people, jackass—I mean, Corporal. Check the tides, too. See you back at the office."

"Yup." Logan bounced back over the edge.

Before going back down the path, Jason took a final look at the bench, the fluttering blanket and the worn basket. He climbed into his brand new oversized truck and headed toward the office.

The truck had been a gift to himself for his fiftieth last spring. When his friends had ribbed him about it, he called it "mid-life crisis prevention," although everyone, including Jason, knew he was way past that. Meanwhile, the truck served the purpose of getting him anywhere at any time, which was part of his job. It also created social opportunities when friends needed the exact type of ridiculous truck they didn't have. Seeing as he was on his third year of being single, these social moments were welcome.

Jason was by no means a dating leper. He had been happily married for the better part of ten years until the relationship devolved, from subtle through cumulative to absolute failure. He and Shawna had married too quickly. She called him the day the divorce papers had arrived at each of their doorsteps. "Diiid weee maaake aaa mistaaaake??" she sobbed into the phone. "No," he replied, teary in his eyes and voice. "No. We loved each other enough to end it." They hung up and he started a three-day bender in equal and opposite reaction to his bullshit statement.

Then Kathy became an immediate staple in his life for eight years. "Good thing we didn't get married," she said one day, kissing him goodbye on the cheek and handing him the keys to the home that was now his alone.

"Good thing," he smiled. He sat on the doorstep as his latest lover-turned-friend drove away, and he remained there well into the night. He took a hiking sabbatical for a week. When he returned, he commenced a dating spree that left him spent, bored, and frightened by the overwhelming variety of woman with whom his friends somehow felt he would be compatible. This was followed by a solo weekend fishing trip. The following Monday, he returned to work with the resolve to cool it for a bit and do a lot of wilderness camping. And maybe get back to painting.

He had showed promise in art classes through grade school. He could draw anything. He drew funny pictures of his buddies and slapped them on the lockers of the girls they liked. At a Paint Night team-building exercise, his colleagues were taken aback by his level of ability, which was blatantly out of place. He felt some shame at not having dumbed it down sufficiently and spent the rest of the night sinking tequila and imitating Magic Mike on the dance floor. This also, he did too well. The evening became the subject of water cooler conversation and office memes for the better part of a year. It wasn't the first time Jason had gone into an evening with absolutely no intention of drawing attention to himself. Like each time before, he was unable to stop once he started. Following Paint Night, he gave up drinking for six months, until his fiftieth birthday, when his staff predictably threw him a surprise party.

As people got hammered at the extravagant hotel suite they had rented, groups and individuals splintered off. Some talked emphatically in corners about things they would never remember. Others descended to smoke outside. Logan curled into an overstuffed chair for a rest, which consisted of appearing to be asleep while commentating loudly on whatever dialogue he caught snippets of. Jason wound up lying on the couch with his head in the lap of his communications agent, Lily. They were good friends. They giggled as she stroked his hair.

"Ya know," he said, "when you and Billy break up, we should get married."

"Jeremy."

"When you and Jeffrey break up, let's get together, we'd have fun."

"Jeremy."

"When you and Jenny break up, we should get together."

"Hahahaha. Jeremy."

"What the fuck is going on?" hollered Jeremy, plowing into the suite. One of the smokers had let him up.

Lily stiffened. Jason was suddenly sober, but chose to play drunk. He rocked himself clumsily into a sitting position. By contrast, his head raced—he had just made Inspector, this shit wasn't okay anymore. Was it ever okay to begin with?

"Hello, Jeremy. Look, I'm sorry about that—"

"I'm gonna punch your fuckin' head off!"

Jason swayed his head from side to side. "No, you're not. I just broke up with someone, Lily was being nice to me. I made a really bad choice there."

Logan's voice floated up from the folds of the chair. "He made a REALLY BAD choice there."

"I don't care," said Jeremy, approaching.

Jason continued. "But if you assault a police officer with another police officer here as a witness, you'd be making a way worse one."

"Waaaaay worse," came Logan's voice. "Nonnnnn-starter."

"Faaaaaak!" screamed Jeremy, waving his tense arms in the air, then dropping them. He shot out his hand toward Lily. "Come on. Let's go. I can't stand the sight of him. I can barely stand the sight of you." Lily and her alcohol consumption stumbled as she rose and left the room.

From Logan's form came, "You made a REALLY BAD choice, Jay-bud."

Jason dropped back down onto the couch and passed out.

"Soooo bad." Logan continued, unaware that his friend was no longer cognizant. "Toooo bad. You an Lilies is cute together."

Jason hauled himself off the couch early the next morning and drove home, his blood thin and his head thick with hangover and self-depreca-tion. His truck's still-new-car smell was sickening. He sat in the drive-way, tapping the steering wheel over and over. What now? What do I do this time?

Once inside the house, he collapsed onto his own couch, and found himself staring at the painting on the wall. It was one he had made some time ago, a wide-angle scene of a river in the woods at sunset. He rose, grabbed the painting, and slammed it on his easel. His gestures slowed and became gentle as he painted tiny silhouettes of two men fishing together in the lower left corner. The negative space still dominated the painting, but its story was entirely different. It was one of repair.

Jason started to breathe again. He lay down on his bed for a nap and woke the next day. He rose and started a new painting. And then another. And another.

The first, a campfire party scene on the beach. Three boys in their late teens, laughing and drinking beer. It is colder; they are wearing coats and toques. One wears a hockey team jacket. Three girls and another boy are further away, dancing next to the water.

> this is Jason's before image of a tragedy where a kid poured a tank of gas on the fire, spilling gas along the way the flame raced back to where someone had parked too close the car exploded, killing three boys, permanently disfiguring the one who had poured the gas

The second, a dining room table, bird's-eye view. Brightly lit, colourful. More like a magazine image than a painting. Beautiful plates adorned with food, glasses full of white wine. An Egyptian-style table cloth. Sets of forearms and hands visible alongside each plate, holding hands in a circle as though someone was saying grace. All wear wedding bands except one, this set of forearms covered in sleeve tattoos.

> this is Jason's before image of a man involved in organized crime who had his hands severed at the wrists he had been a restaurant owner among other things

The third, a background highly reminiscent of the famous crosswalk photo of the Beatles outside Abbey Road, but on a street that could be anywhere. A young woman has just reached the other side.

> this is Jason's before image of a woman struck down at crosswalk in a subdivision by a young driver who was texting while driving
>
> the driver denied this
>
> the date stamps on the threads of the texts denied her based on her near-constant texting history, it had only been a matter of time

These were his first three. Then came dozens of others. He hung a select few, the ones that brought him the greatest peace.

No one knew that he painted on his own time, or how much. Most of the friends who came over didn't notice the canvasses. The ones who did remarked on the quality of the work or the interesting variety of subject matter. No one ever connected the dots.

Logan's number popped up on Jason's phone as he pulled into the station.

"Hey. Deceased picnic lady lived alone. There are two daughters living in town. Want me to notify once we get confirmation from Coro?"

"Please and thanks." Jason picked up his gloves and some paperwork from the front seat. "Take Milligan with you, he needs to work on his nerves for this stuff."

"Hahahaha," laughed Logan's voice. "Right? Gotta stop with the crying. He's getting better, though. At least he can introduce himself now."

"Progress, not perfection." Jason shifted in his posture and tone. "Although we're aiming for perfection. Call me when it's done."

"Yup. Later."

Jason headed into the building on the invisible conveyor belt that carried him past security; past the receptionist of his own department; along the hallways where hung portraits of previous commanding offi-cers, retired or deceased; past the communications office, where Lily still smiled, acknowledged him, and collaborated with excellence, but from a permanent distance; to his admittedly swanky office overlooking the town. The view in the distance was of the beach where the boys had died. And, most recently, Marie Hinckey, age fifty-eight, of Botten Road.

He woke his computer and started to log in. He stopped, fidgeted. He got up and walked to the window. He went to his bookshelf, then walked around his desk. He usually waited until he got home, but not today.

Jason closed his office door. Seated back at his desk, he pulled a piece of paper from his printer and began to sketch.

shoreline, skyline bench, details of the basket's weave
shadows, colours, folds of the blanket   // pause //

tree deadfall appears lightly in the corner of the image   // pause //

an eraser comes for the trees, returns the landscape to
open land and sea and sky   // pause //

enter Marie Hinckey, alive and laughing, seated on the bench
enter the back of a man's head and shoulders, a hint of a smile in profile
a hand on hers, emerging from the cuff of an anorak

Under the Same Moon

Deshane stared up the fifty-foot white wall, taking in the giant banner: 3, it read. Black on white, Helvetica font obnoxious in size, the number reaching from ground to sky. It undulated in the late afternoon breeze, giant slow waves under plastic.

She had been here for about an hour now. *Here* was a query more than a statement. In lieu of the standard bachelor and bachelorette parties, the couple had acquiesced to their wedding party's proposition of Wedding Adventure Weekend, with no detail provided beyond the title. The initial event consisted of her and Noah being separated immediately following the post-rehearsal brunch, blindfolded, and dropped off at different locations.

Here, for Deshane, was an abandoned midway. This particular midway, even in its heyday, would have been considered second-rate, or worse. The derelict games and rides had been hand assembled with scrap materials by someone with questionable measurement ability and underpowered tools. Once-grassy knolls were now puffs of straggly hay. The park's creator had attempted large statues of dinosaurs and, for some reason, a chicken. An uneventful mini putt bled through the centre of the park, its previously green veins now running brown and black. Deshane stood in a little valley that represented the mini putt's epicentre. She bent over a hole and a retrieved a dirty, dented golf ball. A critter had taken an uneven bite out of it.

The people in their wedding party had means—friends in construction, friends in graphic design, friends in catering. The park had been walled off with white privacy tarpaulin. She had the initial impression of being inside a square kilometer of cake, until she looked around. Was this cool or depressing? What kind of arena had Noah been dropped into? Her Apple watch told her nothing except the time. Their wedding party also included a pathologically inclined IT genius. There was a signal blocker somewhere.

She felt disturbed yet safe; they wouldn't put her or her fiancé in harm's way. Her initial surveillance of the ramshackle park complete, she sat down next to the gnawed golf ball and what might have once been a water feature.

3, she thought. Three hours? Three days? She shuddered at three days. That would make sense, though. They were to be married four days from now.

Panic broadened within her. She was a planner. She was on top of every detail of her wedding preparations, and her friends knew that. But now … no chance to double check her double-checked lists, no chance to pack her own bag for the night-before-the-wedding party, no chance to call her sister or her aunts. Surely they had accounted for all that. Gah. Planning is the enemy of adventure, no? Deshane loved both planning *and* adventure, when those worlds didn't collide. At this very moment, she didn't love either.

My tan will be that much nicer, she thought. She turned her face to the sun, breathing deeply and listening to the hot August wind in the overgrown grass. She could hear traffic on a highway close by. Logistics returned to her thoughts with a manifest—they must have left me some food, somewhere to sleep.

She rose and began a more organized acquaintanceship with the park. She came across a small army-like tent set up behind a bent water slide. The tent was neatly laid out with a cot, pillow, and blanket. Nice bedding. There was a book on the bed with a pen beside it. A sticker across the cover read:

Bad Choices, Secrets, and Ghosts
Deshane's Confessional Graveyard

Really. So they've added a nosy twist. And they think they're funny.

She dropped the journal back on the cot, the pen bouncing in disorganized counterpoint. Beside the tent was a small shelter with a bar fridge and a microwave plugged into an extension cord of suspect condition that was popping up from the ground. The fridge was crammed with veggie trays and other snacks, along with a couple of bottles of her favourite white. Deshane felt a smile transform her face. Comforts.

She knelt beside a large rectangular picnic basket. Dishes, cutlery, flashlights, chips, and crackers. A small tin box, the kind that contained a geometry set when she was a kid. This one held a small baggie of white powder, a short straw, and another baggie with what appeared to be two joints in it.

WTF.

She smelled the baggie with the joints—the bright, skunky odour was legit. The powder can't be ... or is it? She closed the tin box and opened the Doritos, which served to attenuate her escalating sensations of weirdness. They know it's not my thing, she thought. They also know that I can take it, that I can handle a challenge, that I can deal with all this shit.

Her quarters were okay. She had done enough budget travelling all over the world to know these were pretty good digs. She rotated on her heels and set off to explore the rest of the grounds. She found her mindset had shifted to that of being stuck in some bougie version of Survivor. Was there a riddle? Were there other things she was supposed to find? Maybe. Maybe not. Three days. Had they at least left her a book? As in, a real book that she could read, not one she was expected to write garbage in?

What the hell was Noah looking at right now?

Maybe it was time for some wine. Or maybe it wasn't. It was all still a bit weird, and she wasn't that much of a drinker. She definitely wasn't into the other stuff. Did Noah get all the same gear? No doubt he did, right down to the blow and the journal.

So if someone gave me three days and no schedule ... what would I do? Deshane laughed out loud. Absolutely not this. She would run, though, which had been her plan prior to finding herself in the back of an SUV and driven around for some time before being deposited here. She still had no idea where she was. A visual sweep of the area now had her thinking Valley. This made sense. The whole area had been a going concern of a tourist trap in the swinging 70s, prior to going bust in the fickle 80s. Her mind ran images of retro TV commercials for the big commercial park her childhood friends had always gone to with their families. This certainly was not it.

Still, her wedding peeps had left her creature comforts, the greatest of which was the space to run. She began to trot, smiling as she took in the whole of the park. It was about to become an obstacle course. Her junior high track and field star-self radiated with excitement as she picked up her pace.

After the run, she discovered plenty of bottled water and facecloths, but no shower. Three days was going to be long that way, but at least there was no one else to offend. She amused herself with a high-end snack of nice cheeses and deli meats, a short meditation session, and the start of sunset. Normally, she didn't get to bed much before midnight; normally, she wasn't contained in a forsaken midway. There was nothing really to do aside from writing in the emotional bait journal, for which she had no plans or content. This was due to her being okay. Better than okay. She had no regrets to date and nothing she wouldn't tell the best friend she was about to marry. It would have been Gwendolyn's idea, the journal. She had known Gwendolyn since grade school. Gwen had been a shit disturber even then, which was lots of fun as long as you were watching the action from the outside.

Before retiring to the tent, Deshane lay on the ground in the centre of the mini putt for a time. The wind had subsided. All the stars were out, in depths and layers she and Noah could never see from their condo balcony in the city. The moon was a perfect gibbous. Three days, she thought. I can do this. And my Noah. We're under the same moon. They always said this to each other on the phone or by text when one of them was away.

We're under the same moon.

This light touches you, too.

She could hear his voice wishing her, "'Night, Desi." He was the only person she had ever allowed to use a short form of her name. Her heart warmed with love for him and with anticipation of their wedding.

In the morning, the same moon glowed a translucent white against a flawless blue sky. Deshane woke abruptly from the briefest of sleeps. She felt like crap. It was an entirely whacked experience, sleeping alone in an abandoned midway in the middle of she wasn't sure where. There were animals moving in the dark, she had heard rustling and screeching nearby—foxes, perhaps. Aside from the odd truck on the highway, she hadn't heard any human activity. She wasn't sure if that was a positive or not.

Coming out into the sun, Deshane looked around and shook her head at the ridiculousness of where she was. It made even less sense now. All appeared as she had remembered from the day before except for the fifty-foot banner. A new one had been unfurled over the wall sometime in the night, an elongated 2.

Creepy, she thought. But it means someone has been here, and it's someone I know. She turned toward the fridge and picnic basket.

Day 2 evolved so slowly she wondered if time was passing at all. She explored the semi-structures to the greatest possible extent without tearing her hands apart on broken surfaces or stepping in something questionable. She ran her new obstacle course twice. Then a third time. What was Noah doing? Was he having any fun? She couldn't say that she was having fun. She was definitely having an experience, and she chose to conceptualize it that way. Anything else was too disturbing.

The Day 2 sunset, when it finally arrived, was beautiful and calming. Its pinks and oranges and blues were framed by the open flaps of the tent where Deshane sat, mentally revising the details of her impending wedding day. She imagined the guests that were coming. From her side, they were mostly friends from school and her aunts who had raised her into adulthood. Her parents had died within a short time of one another just before she graduated high school. Her dad went first, of brain cancer. Two years later, her mother acted on the forethought to assist herself out of a rapid, early-onset dementia. Deshane had come into the world with an independent streak, her character and practicality well established prior to her parents' decline and death. Her character had been a source of pride for them, for her.

They were transparent figures at this point. Their spirits moved in and out of her heart and chest on their own transcendental schedules, occupying variable amounts of weight and space there. She did not imagine, except in fleeting sketches, their involvement in her wedding preparation and day. She took comfort in the understanding of their essence, while feeling overwhelmed with gratitude for the friends and family she had around her now.

Although not right right now.

Right now, her friends were all somewhere with indoor plumbing, air conditioning, and her wedding details. Deshane laughed, then felt irritated. This is supposed to be fun, this is supposed to be a party. She looked around at the dry landscape of weirdness.

Fuck it.

She marched to the fridge and unscrewed the cap from a bottle of wine. She looked for a glass, then shook her head. Flinging the cap over her shoulder, she tipped the bottle upward and felt an inner rejoicing at the cool, vibrant liquid. It seeped through her core, melting the anxiety she had experienced more often than not for the past twenty-four hours. She felt increasingly in the mood of someone about to get married rather than someone carried off and now living in an abandoned theme park, somehow by her own assent.

By dark, the three flashlights she had found were swinging from tree branches, rigged up with twine she had discovered at the bottom of the picnic basket. She sang some of her favourite songs and danced around a bit. She was a good dancer. She had taken classes as a kid, but soccer had won the adolescent competition for her time and attention. The dance moves leapt out of a recessed drawer in her mind; she would bring them full-on to the dance floor of the wedding reception. She crashed on the cot, gazing out at the stars, and then rolled over onto an uncomfortable small boxy thing she recalled to be the journal.

Fuck you, she thought, flinging the journal out of the tent. Not everyone is a goddamn liar or cheat or thief or unintegral asshole. I'm not perfect, but I got nothin' for you, Gwendolyn Figaro. Neither does my guy.

Or does he?

Deshane realized she had never really pondered this. She'd never had reason to. The journal landed out of sight, but her mind's eye read its branding over and over. Confessional, my ass. She turned herself toward the moon. It was brighter than before. All the brighter for you, too, my love, she said softly. Under the same bright moon.

Wine made the night pass with greater ease relative to the previous one, but it delivered an edgy morning. The ambient temperature was already hotter than it had been the two days previous. Deshane drained and ditched two bottles of water and was halfway through her third before she thought to turn in the direction of the banner.

1.

The image was ridiculous, the anemic number pointed toward the sky. Or was it pointed toward the ground. Whatever.

While not totally hung over, Deshane hated any degree of hung over. Her friends had politely intuited sports drinks among the fridge contents. Two laps of the obstacle course and a short nap later, she felt a bit better physically, but remained agitated in spirit. I want out. Now. I want my life back. Now. For a moment, she felt she would never get to leave. She yanked herself back from that cliff. Can't be. That's not what this is. I agreed to this, sort of. He misses me as much as I miss him. The poor boy doesn't do solitary anywhere near as well as I do.

Her agitation had her pacing. Pacing, pacing, pacing over and over along the running course she had established. Actually, I didn't ask for this. Whose idea WAS this? Why didn't I just go for the stupid penis straws and princess outfit. If I ever do this again—wait.

I'm never doing this again.

She exhaled slowly, some tension gone. She loved him. Two days until their wedding. It was going to be a blast. Let the time pass. It will pass. This will pass.

She lay in the tent for a while. The time of day manufactured some shade from the wrecked slide and the one surviving tree on the property. Waking suggested to her that she must have slept again, even though the sun showed no visible advancement. From her horizontal perspective on the cot, her eyes landed on a shape in the distance, a second horizon among the long grasses. Its shape was that of an oversized matchbox that might have once been orange and green. Curiosity lifted her and walked her toward it.

The leggy 1 loomed to her left. To her right, a shattered House of Mirrors returned distorted pieces of herself through its long-discarded door. She was startled by her lack of torso, her removed left leg. The top of her head ran wild. She thought of her wedding stylist, who was beyond excited about her Caribbean springs. Deshane had always loved her hair. Seeing it as an erratic creature separated from her core was jarring.

Get a grip. You're fine.

She approached the box with its slanted top and holes. It's a Whack-a-Mole, she thought, a shitty one, a kid's project or an alcoholic wet dream. The holes were barely circular and they varied in diameter. She knew of the game but had no recollection of ever playing it. Memories of her parents' voices spread insidious. Amusement parks and fairs were not in their repertoire of fun, and she could feel their dismissal, the people and rides coated with a film of distain. She felt her own distant but familiar desire to see the spinning lights, to drive bumper cars. It was nothing she insisted on as a child, or even thought to, but now that this window of her life was nailed shut, she recalled something beyond it she never knew she wanted so badly.

Was this the fucking confession? They gave me a journal, they want a confession. I have zero salacious encounters, no rides in the back of cop cars, no waking up somewhere in Vegas. Just a goddamn stupid Whack-a-Mole. I never got to play Whack-a-Mole.

Deshane kicked at the dead game. The frustration in her burgeoned. It spilled from her stomach into her heart and limbs. Her arms flailed as she kicked harder. This was insufficient. She screamed in rage and flew through the grounds looking for a weapon, something she could swing at the box to finish it off. A snapped metal arm gleamed at her from the ground a few feet away. Her hands ripped at the grass until she pried the bar loose from where it had been scarred over by the earth. She ran back to the game and smashed at it over and over, until there was no more game. The box was now an open pile of disorganized rubbish. The rotten wooden top was demolished, the asymmetric holes dissolved into splinters. She howled and tossed the bar aside.

What the fuck is happening. She stomped around. This isn't me.

She turned back to the game, apology in her heart and on her lips. I'm sorry, she said quietly. It's not your fault. Someone gave a shit about you once.

She willed herself back into her senses, directing her full attention to the details of the mess in front of her.

What is that?

In what had been the far-left corner of the now destroyed box, a round shape was exposed. It was the colour of expired cotton candy, although it couldn't be that. Any form of cotton candy would be long evaporated or consumed by wildlife. Aware that her hands were a bit roughed from the metal bar, and caring not to worsen them, she carefully picked away at the wooden shards until she excavated a round plastic lid. With a stick, she scraped the debris and earth away from the container and eventually lifted it from the dirt. Folgers, she determined from the disintegrating wrap of the large tin coffee can. Mountain Roast. The font and can were old. Memories and feelings rushed through her from more TV commercials she had watched as a kid.

Fuck. Not more memories.

She brushed off the lid, clenched her teeth in anticipation of terrible, and opened the can.

Nothing leapt out at her, aside from the sight of rolls of carefully bundled cash. Dozens of them. Mostly large bills. Her eyes widened. She pushed around gently at the rolls with the stick. What the hell. She looked around to see if she could spot cameras anywhere. She couldn't. She remembered Heath saying, "No cameras, no worries!" as they guided her out of the car. Had Noah heard the same message where he was?

A yellowed but well-preserved piece of paper, folded accordion-like, hugged the periphery of the can. She placed the can on the ground and withdrew the paper. The script was juvenile and jagged, written by someone who had to work hard at it. It read:

> If you find this money it's mine. Put it Back Because I am coming Back for it Soon. I could be Coming Back right now. Whatever you do don't give it to Danny Burke he can't have it he may say it's his it's not. put it Back and pretend you didn't find it OR ELSE

Deshane guesstimated the can to have been placed there in the mid to late 80s. Was buddy really coming back? Doubt it. Yet … she re-read the note and felt nauseous and thrilled at the same time. Was he Coming Back right now? Or right now?

She looked around. She looked up at the 1.

Doubt it.

She sat cross-legged beside the can and counted. And counted. And counted again. There was almost thirty thousand dollars. The bills were old-school, and she guessed them to be of about the same era as the closing of the park. She recounted. She checked her watch. It was 3:47 p.m. "You're not real," she said to her watch. "You're not real," she said to the money. Caught up in the unanticipated thrall, she rolled the can and lid around in the dust to remove fingerprints. She clasped the accordion note by her newly flawed fingernails and returned it to the can. With her knuckles, she replaced the can in its long-established home in the dirt, tamped it down and covered it with more dirt and shards. She headed back to her tent carrying a big, loose ball of hundreds and fifties.

She opened the fridge. She contemplated the remaining bottle of wine. She closed the fridge. She opened the picnic basket. The tin of the geometry set caught her eye as had the lid of the coffee tin from its battered nest. She closed the picnic basket. She walked down to the middle of the mini putt, which had established itself as her comfort zone within the midway. She sat, lost in years and thoughts, until the sun set. Then she went to bed without eating or drinking.

When she awoke, she was clear of mind and spirit. She ran her course and ate the healthy food that remained. The banner did not read 0; it had disappeared altogether. Now to wait.

It took most of the day for them to arrive, which they finally did in a gale-force cavalcade of cars and cargo trucks. Her entire wedding party burst through the white perimeter wrap. Her friends rushed forward, laughing and hugging her. A bunch of teens ran in at dizzying speed and set up a DJ booth and PA, racks of lighting, and a catering station. She recognized the kids from the football team that Noah coached.

Noah's friends walked him in. His face was wan and he was working to be jovial, but he lit up when he saw her. They rushed into each other's arms, overjoyed with familiarity, proximity, smells, textures, and love that was all the more amped up for these past three days of bizarre separation.

The sun was setting. Tunes started up and a rave-worthy lightshow blazed against the remaining white-wrapped walls of the park, a display of colours, swirls, giant patterns of stars, and a gobo that projected "d&n4ev." All Deshane wanted was to leave the park with Noah, although she had to admit that the scene beyond his shoulder was spectacular. The park was transformed by technology and the warmth of the people she loved. It was smart, creative, and beautiful, like the friends who had put it together.

Deshane pulled back and looked at Noah. He was still smiling.

"You look … are you okay?" she asked. Something twigged in her mind. "Did you do … any of that shit?"

His gentle, forthcoming features tightened for a split atom of time that would have been imperceptible to anyone else. "No!" he said, drawing her close. She could no longer see his face. "And this has been crazy. We're never doing this again!" He laughed. Despite the jagged bolt that shot briefly through her heart, she relaxed fully into him, receiving the restoration of who they had always been.

"I can't wait to fully be together. I can't wait to have kids." His voice was emotional.

This is top of mind for him right now?

Heather tapped her on the shoulder. Deshane pulled away, to be handed her overnight bag. "We packed this for you," said Heather, unable to contain her self-satisfaction. "Go back to the tent and get changed. Lots of wipes in there, too." She laughed. "This is your Wedding Adventure PARTY!"

Noah and Deshane clasped hands, then let go. She smiled back over her shoulder at him on her way to the tent. She closed its flaps and opened her bag. At the top was a journal identical to the one she had, with Noah's name on it instead of her own. She flipped through to find it just as empty, even the slightest bit emptier. One sheet had been precisely torn out midway through the book. That's curious, she thought. Who knows what he needed that for.

She placed the two journals side by side on the cot. The fractional wobble in Noah's face flashed through her mind. What happened to him? What does it mean?

Does it even matter?

She took the pillow from her cot, reached into the pillowcase, and transferred the vintage bills into her overnight bag.

Her friends knew her well and had packed exactly what she would have packed for herself. She took her time dressing for the party. She opened her compact mirror and instantly snapped it shut again, choosing to head out without makeup. As she tossed the compact back into her bag, the journals looked up at her.

Bad Choices, Secrets, and Ghosts

At what point exactly did the present moment become a bad choice, a secret, a ghost?

She placed the bag under the cot as though it had always belonged there, and strode out under the moon.

I, II, III,
Noah

His available senses informed him that the room was big. It was also somewhat cold. There was the sound of industrial air flow. He listened to footsteps, three sets decisive (his friends) and one set tentative (his own), the sound bouncing off vertical surfaces. The party slowly mounted a set of stairs (five, counted Noah) and moved another fifteen paces before he was instructed to sit.

Noah lowered himself to the floor. Heath's voice told him to wait until he heard a door shut very clearly, and then to open his eyes. "No cameras, no worries!" came final words as three pairs of feet carried Noah's groomsmen away from him. It seemed a long time before a crash bar signaled the opening of a metal door that took its time to shut. The clang and boom faded. He fingered the blindfold that was mostly plastered to his forehead and eyelids with sweat. He felt hesitation in removing it, although he was sure it would be fine, that *he* would be fine. These were his friends. Their friends.

As part of their Wedding Adventure Weekend, he and Deshane (Desi, to him only) had attended a brunch with their wedding party. They were subsequently blindfolded and dropped off at separate locations with no further information such as where they were or for how long. How far away is she from me? Noah took a deep breath and removed the blindfold.

He was sitting cross-legged on a stage in a performance theatre that appeared to double as a movie house, one he had never been in. He wasn't a big theatre-goer to begin with. It was mid-sized, he figured, its capacity about 350. The rows of seats he sat facing were a shade of please-refurbish-me teal, once matched by the lesser-worn rectangular sound treatment panels that hung on the walls. He rose and cautiously began to explore.

Behind him, just beyond centre stage, was a cot with nice bedding and pillows. Between him and the cot was an unfamiliar object. Its base was rectangular in shape, approximately the height of a fire hydrant, and the top was a dial that resembled something between a giant chicken knob from a guitar amplifier and the needle of a sun dial. The base was a deep mahogany and the dial a distressed beige, treated to look a century old or more. The dial had five possible settings, based on the Roman numerals burnt into the base. It was set to I. There was some resistance as he wrapped both hands around the knob to move it. He put it through its paces, through to V and back. Nothing happened save for the sound of the clicking into each place. He descended from the stage to check out the rest of the area.

He found important things that slightly eased his anxiety, including a small staff room with a kitchenette, and a bathroom. A hospitality-type arrangement had been left for him. There was a basket full of chips, crackers, and other dry goods. He tentatively opened the fridge, as he tentatively opened any fridge that was new to him, and smiled. Lots and lots of beer. Bottled water. A bottle of Desi's favourite white wine. Three vegetable trays and one fruit tray. Some fancy-looking sandwiches. Wait. How much food is here for me and for how long? What about a warm dinner? He opened the freezer in hopes of microwavable things, and was relieved to find three boxed entrées. Three nights, maybe? He sighed. His system pulsed with novelty, which he knew would likely wear off sooner than later. Oh well. My choice to agree to this, he thought as his gaze shifted to a rectangular tin box on the freezer door shelf. Something that might be a geometry set? Why put that in the freezer? The box chilled the tips of his fingers as he opened it.

A baggie of white powder and three perfectly rolled joints sat neatly arranged in lieu of protractors and compasses. He was surprised but not.

This must be Grant's idea. They had one crazy party in university and Grant never stopped talking about it. My choice to NOT agree to this. He returned the tin and shut the freezer door. Wait, is Desi getting all the same stuff? Or mostly the same stuff? I don't know that she's ever even done that kind of thing. Panic ignited in his chest. What if she tries it and goes apeshit and hurts herself? Shit. No. She wouldn't. Not her thing. Definitely not her thing.

He got a hold of his breathing and wandered out to discover a tiny ticket office and canteen. The windowpanes of the main entrance had been covered over with heavy newsprint and glue. He guessed it might be early evening. The late August light was pushing hard against its newsprint barrier, trying but not quite able to tell him the time. Now highly mindful of time, he raised his wrist, but his watch was blank. They had blocked more than just the cell signal somehow. Grant, again—he had always been a little weird. He was funny, and a vault for stuff he wasn't supposed to know or re-tell, but weird.

The cot called him as a home base. He returned to it and gauged its yield as he sat, making sure it would hold his dense linebacker's body. It did. He looked out once again out at the seats. Putting his hand on the pillow, he felt a hard object beneath it. He retrieved a journal with a sticker across the cover:

Bad Choices, Secrets, and Ghosts
Noah's Confessional Graveyard

You've gotta be kidding me. He snorted with laughter. That had to come from Amy or Gwendolyn or someone. It reeks of girl drama. My choice to NOT write in that. There would be a pen, though. Where's the pen? He reached a bit further under the pillow to find it. It announced its place of origin, a hotel in New Hampshire. Random. He placed the pen on the floor beside the cot and held the journal in both hands. It felt like his only contact with a semblance of people, his people, even though the journal idea was lame. What were they hoping for there? His brow knit just as the lights snapped off, firing his adrenaline in the total darkness. "Whoa!" he blurted.

A split second later, the three stage walls around him lit up in ceiling-to-floor white. He traced the source upward to three projectors mounted on the ceiling. A massive number 3, black on white, appeared on each wall. He turned to face the projectionist booth at the back of the theatre. It appeared to be unattended. His friends were too smart, they had rigged this up remotely. Impressive, yet insane. Three, though ... three days? He recalled the food situation. Likely. He and Desi would be married on the fourth. He smiled, despite the anxiety that had been bouncing around in his blood over the last half hour. He loved her. He would leave here to be with her. He could manage this.

The screens went black, as did the room. In the few seconds that his eyes began to adjust, all three screens lit up with larger-than-life porn.

You've gotta be kidding me.

Like most adults, Noah was neither a stranger nor immune to porn, but it had been a while since their last encounter. This manifestation of it was overwhelming. Everything was five times larger and louder than it was ever meant to be. You've gotta be kidding me, he thought again. How long will this go on? Is this my next three days? And nights? This is so not me. Do they know me at all? Or maybe that's the point. Will they shut it off at night? He sat for some time in disbelief, unable to process the sensory overload. Fuck sakes. He shook his head and headed to the kitchen for a beer and less volume.

This can't be Desi's sitch, too. Or can it? Fuck me. Three fucking days.

Noah lit into a bag of chips. Then another. He sank the first beer and cracked open a second. The porn barrage continued in the main room. He reviewed the space in his mind, then headed for the dial in the centre of the stage. Maybe it has a function now.

On the walls, two unfit but well-groomed men arrived, shirtless, in a furniture delivery van at the door of a lower middle class suburban home. One of them knocked and shouted, "Mrs. Delahunty?" Mrs. Delahunty opened the door, clearly just out of the bath.

Nope, thought Noah. He put his beer down beside the platform and turned the knob to II.

The gargantuan visuals and sound now filled the walls with My Little Pony.

His reaction to the contrast was visceral. He felt the closest he had come to passing out since a concussion from rec football two years ago. What the fuck. He felt sideways yet relieved. He stood watching the stage left screen. Fantasia was about to perform her dressage show for the first time ever in front of her parents. The other ponies were so encouraging, so positive! He warmed a bit from the more heartfelt message of it, but then his heart sank again as he found himself mouthing the dialogue. He remembered the episode. He remembered it well, having watched it over and over during the time in his late twenties where he had taken in season after season of the show. He had collections. He had gone to conferences. He had been a Brony.

Had been.

They don't know about that.

No fuckin way. Do they know about that? Desi sure as hell didn't.

He felt terrified.

They said no cameras. But I'll bet you a thousand dollars they're tracking what I watch, he thought. Noah wheeled back to the knob. III.

Bridgerton.

Seriously?

The show had essentially been Desi's porn and perhaps, partly, his, during one of the pandemic shutdowns. That was about all it was good for, though.

The ridiculousness of the whole set-up was mounting in the form of frustration and physical discomfort. Whose idea was this of fun? He was having no fun. It was distressing, even. Is Desi having any fun? Is she stuck in some bizarre, distressful situation, or is she at a spa somewhere? He went back to the dial. Where's the TSN, boys? Please let IV be TSN. Or a power off.

IV was far worse. Channels I through III smashed on to each of the three walls surrounding the stage, all running at once. The audio and video were loud, competing, cumulative. Noah felt disoriented and claustrophobic. It was too stimulating, too many worlds and eras colliding. He was about to grab the bedding and go set it up in the kitchenette when he figured he may as well try V. It'll stop. It has to make it stop. Please.

Everything went black. His ears rang slightly at the absence of cacophonic audio from the fucked-up mix of sources. The sound of rapid, shallow breathing slowly started to come from within him instead of from outside of him. His eyes adjusted to the house lights, set to a semi-comforting level. He dropped down on the bed, determined to pull himself together. He realized he needed strategy.

What would satisfy this stupid bachelor party's organizing committee while not making him lose his mind? What could he manufacture so he would have something to tell Desi that wasn't a complete lie? Were they even going to be telling each other about this? Of course they were, they told each other everything. Or, now that he thought about it, just short of everything.

They had agreed, no strippers. Noah shook his head. He wouldn't be lying—this was somehow worse. Those fuckers.

It's okay to leave this off for a bit while I think.

Noah headed back to the kitchenette. He chose water over beer. In the tiny foyer, he sat down on the broken tile floor amid a few dust bunnies and a warped brown rubber doorstop, facing the only semblance of real light that he had. He wished he knew what time it was. He wished he was with Desi. Their life was nice and mostly predictable and fun.

Three days. The sun is setting. I can do this.

He wrestled his breath to evenness as Desi had taught him, and as he had since taught all his Phys Ed students and the teams he coached at school.

We chose this adventure over the regular engagement party shit, thinking we were cool somehow. This isn't cool. I need to be cool, more in spite of the moment than because of it.

Noah headed back into the theatre to fetch the bedding. As he lifted the cot, the journal slapped to the floor.

Bad Choices, Secrets, and Ghosts

He left it there. He carried the cot to the kitchenette, dumped it beside the kitchen counter, and returned to the stage. There, he inhaled deeply and hauled the knob back to the first position. The porn started up again.

There was nothing he could do about the volume, but at least he could dull it some and get away from the images by living in the kitchenette. He microwaved a pizza. One dinner down, two to go. On the walls of the stage, people fucked for hours. And hours and hours and hours.

We're not this, thought Noah. He curled himself under the covers on the cot, which was just undersized for him and now wedged between two countertops in a kitchenette that was built in an age of smaller people. My Desi. Me and Desi in T-minus two microwave dinners. Wow. I'm measuring the duration of my bachelor party-of-one by microwaved dinners. I know she's waiting, too. Sleep as a defence? He estimated it to be approximately 9 p.m. Early. Neither he nor his partner were early-to-bed types.

He sat bolt upright in the cot. Introduce a masking variable.

Noah would have gone for statistics over physical education if he had been better at school. He had a terrible time reading, but his head ran numbers all the time: sports stats, counting of objects, multiplying 3-digit numbers by 3-digit numbers, mentally measuring items and spaces in his head and then challenging himself by actually measuring them. The measurement results were uncanny and satisfying more often than not.

He returned to the dial and rotated it to V. The quiet was a form of relief that was near erotic in and of itself. He sat back down on the stage with the intention to mediate. Prior to his eyes closing, they started to measure the space. If he ran the two exterior aisles as well as the middle one, plus one length of the stage with the stairs on either side, it would give him approximately 700 metres, for which his usual pace would be about two minutes per kilometre, which he would slow for the purpose of this marathon.

Close enough.

As long as he counted off the same number of laps per channel, the amount of time on each would be close enough as to nullify what could be construed as a preference. They would be disappointed. They would have nothing on him. No one was to have anything on him.

Meditation could wait. He could give himself V later to assure a few hours of sleep. They couldn't fault him that. He rose, moved the dial to I, and started jogging out the masking interval for each channel.

✳

Noah awoke. He had crashed out at some point. Sore from the cramped sleeping arrangement, he contemplated moving the cot back to the stage. Then he thought not.

He estimated he had put in a good two hours rotating the dial, running, masking. But how could he really be sure? He didn't know how long he had been asleep, either.

What he did know was that there was no shower in the theatre. His wedding party had probably not banked on him running almost non-stop for the duration of his stay. This is regrettable, he thought, ducking his head into his shirt and smelling it. At least I'm alone. I don't want to be alone, though.

Images of Deshane flooded his mind, his heart. Soon I won't be.

He discovered some instant coffee and a kettle. He thought of the dial. What if I just leave it off altogether? He wasn't good with silence. Let's see, though. Maybe I can be?

Without the din of the production on stage, everything else was somehow louder. The microwave was loud, the spoon in the mug was loud, his drinking was loud, his breathing was loud. He didn't make it through his coffee before moving the switch back to I.

Three women, each fifteen feet high on the screens with breasts nearly as wide, were naked and heading for a pool boy. A kid too young to be in porn. So many of them are too young to be in porn. Noah started his circuit.

The numbers spread, a slow infection in his head. The seats multiplied as he tapped them while running up the left aisle, then the right aisle. The number of seats per row was inconsistent, necessitating extra calculation. He chose another measure of time in the form of how many of his own footsteps he heard going up each aisle at each pass. He counted the number of cracks in the wood near to the centre edge of the stage, the number of acoustical panels on each side—there was one less on the left, they were spaced slightly wider—the distance between stains on the aisle carpets. It began to be too much to keep in his mind.

He had calculated food and washroom breaks to line up with the My Little Pony segments. These were beyond incompatible with everything else. They elicited a deep emotional response from a banished part of his life. At the next II, he started the mental clock of his break and leapt up onto the stage. He picked up the pen and the journal, and delicately tore a page from what he estimated to be its exact centre (he would later count the blank pages to verify). He sat and began to write the stats. He would only use one page, hoping no one would find it missing. He wrote smaller and smaller. He filled the page, then turned it over and wrote more. When both sides were filled, he resumed running.

By the time he felt he should eat something for supper, he was starting to feel unhappy and depleted. He had surfed the waves of exercise-induced elation and misery, with misery starting to win out. Two more days. One-point-five days? He walked out to the opaque front doors. The sun had set. His legs were still, but his brain was running running running with numbers. As he trotted back toward the stage to switch to III, his calf seized in a forceful cramp.

"Fuck!" he yelled.

He crashed down into one of the theatre seats. What's with this. The nutrition his friends had provided was fine for watching a ridiculous amount of TV, but not for what he wound up doing. No one had planned on that. He drilled his empty water bottle across the room.

My Little Pony carried on in three one-dimensional squares in front of him. Noah's resigned heart registered shame, peace, and excitement. He registered the datedness of the video production. He had braved the telling of his hobby one time, maybe ten years ago, to a woman he had met up with for a first date. She had seemed soft, like she might not judge him. It was a calculated risk; his hobby, too, was soft, a means of comfort and escapism, of making the world gentler. It was a way of lifting his spirits when he felt lonely. Her revulsion had destroyed him. This reveal experiment did not bear repeating—it rang the alarm of adulthood. It was time for him to move on and for no one to ever discover this. He worked with kids, he had a talent for coaching. When he saw this part of his world from the outside, he despised himself for not having quashed it sooner. And then there was Desi. A strong, self-made force of nature. She would have no time for this. No one would have time for this. No one except the other Bronies, but they weren't going to provide him a life mate or a paycheque. He dropped his collection in piles of black plastic bags next to a charity bin late one night. He deleted his email account and threw himself into weightlifting. His doctor yet again recommended antidepressants. He started part-time courses toward a business degree, where he met Deshane, in accounting class.

When had he started counting, came the question. Counting and accounting were not the same thing.

For as long as I can remember, came the response.

Shit, the time—

He shot out of his seat toward the stage, dragging his seized leg behind him. The dial switched, he dropped beside it. He was a goal-driven being, and his current and only goal was to fully disappoint his wedding party's lewd voyeuristic event. Men. We can be pretty fucking horrible.

Lord Bridgerton was about to give Hastings the what-for on account of messing with his sister. What a dolt, thought Noah. Just let her be her own person. Knowing that His and Her Grace would be just fine, Noah stretched out on the stage and closed his eyes. He began another run of numbers, shorter, soothing, in the form of a paced breathing exercise.

When he awoke, he knew his masking variable was thrown, with no idea by how long. He cranked the dial to IV and let the shitshow run its course. He hauled his exhausted body to the kitchenette. He tore his scrawling stats sheet in two, wet each section under the sink, and inserted them into his ears. He downed a beer, smashed the bottle into the sink with the others, and curled up on the cot for an undetermined length of time. Sleep was there, not there. His dreams were a mess, but nothing compared to that ongoing in the other room.

His internal clock struck a new hour. Post-game. He rose from the cot, removed his makeshift earplugs and flushed them down the toilet. He picked up the broken glass from the sink and carried the cot back to centre stage. He silenced the production and sat until his friends arrived. He estimated they would arrive shortly, which is exactly when they did.

St. Lucia

"**R**emember when we used to 'go out' for drinks?" laughed Rob as he fanned the cards out to his Friday night poker gang.

They laughed. "Like when we 'hung out' in bars?" asked Andrew.

Everyone ordered and re-ordered their cards, smiling to themselves and silently recalling a myriad of moments that used to be called *hanging out in bars*. They had visions of sitting at tables or at the bar itself, memories of packed crowds, of small groups, of quiet pints. They recalled arriving solo, leaving in duo, stumbling out at closing. Some people they remembered well, some belonged to seas of dancing bodies without names.

"I'm going for it," said Lacey, pushing in all her chips. Lacey had absolutely no poker face. She leaned back in self approval, then admired her beer. Her features softened with nostalgia. "Remember Rey's?"

A collective sigh. "Rey's …" several said in chorus.

"Holy shit," said Fletch. "What a time."

Outwardly, they occupied Rob's kitchen. Inwardly, they were all back at Rey's Tavern, always with the Jamiroquai and the Tragically Hip and the Slowcoaster, late afternoon light crossfading into dimmed bar light and eventually out into streetlight. Smoking had been banned by then, but would never completely disappear from the rectangular lungs of the low-ceilinged building. They all had their pictures within the collage under the glass of the 30-foot bar, capturing sundry states of inebriation. 'Home of the Fifty Cent Fifty' was Rey's slogan for Labatt-sponsored Happy Hour on Thursday nights, which was, unsurprisingly, a weekly debacle of stupidity performed on repeat by throngs of twenty-somethings.

"Man. We had nothing to do and nothing to lose," laughed Rob.

"Your play." Lacey nudged Fletch. "You might have something to lose. Again."

A wicked snowstorm surged outside. The houses across the road were barely visible tonight, during a month where yet another wave of the pandemic had subsided just enough to permit multiple household gatherings. The weekly poker game had resumed after the better part of a year.

"Rey's. That's a blast from the past," whistled Andrew, tapping the table.

Rob sailed a card toward him. "You bartended," he said to Lacey. "Jesus. What was that like?"

The players withdrew into themselves. Some giggled, some exhaled loudly as they re-lived images of their own crazy times and imagined the next level insanity that Lacey must have seen. Lacey smiled, her own highlight reel blazing. "Pretty nuts. But it depended how much you bought into all the bar life bullshit, or if you stuck around too long after closing."

Different images started to appear to her. Bloodied knuckles. Broken faces. Women leaving in states they shouldn't have with men they shouldn't have. Men who thought they owned the world already, then somehow felt they owned it more as alcohol and drugs elevated their privilege, fuelled the greed. How had she managed to swerve the worst of it? She was sizeable, she was loud. The boss wasn't concerned about her closing up on her own. She had never pondered that. Maybe she didn't come across as prey material.

"Remember Lucy?" asked Fletch.

Lucy, whose full name was Lucia.

Lacey chuckled. "Yeah. We worked a lot together. She was fun."

She recalled that Rey wasn't concerned about Lucy closing up on her own because he always took those shifts, too.

"Were any of you guys there the night she got up all of the sudden and started singing backup with Epping, and the bass player was like, who the hell is that, and he went to throw her off the stage but she sounded so awesome the singer shoved him back and she wound up doing the whole show?"

Andrew folded, recalling a back-alley blowjob to the sound of the third set. "That was awesome."

Rob shook his head. All assumed it was in response to his own recollection of the craziness of that evening, or perhaps to the sluggish pace of the card game. Inwardly, he was shaking off unwelcome memories of heavy, lurching, drunken sadness. His body was recalling it far more acutely than his thoughts. He felt himself swaying at the back of the room with the feeling of not knowing a soul, even though he knew everyone there. Drinking too much had always brought him to the edge of the horrible hole of self-effacement. He had a tipping point, which often got tipped at Rey's. There had been rare occasions when he would see it coming and fend it off by going home. Six Jäger shooters plus an incalculable amount of draft didn't fend off anything except well-being.

"Anyone here ever go to St. Lucia?" asked a grinning Fletch.

"St. Lucia?" asked Andrew, knowing full well but not admitting.

Rob feigned indifference, not wanting to admit that he didn't know what Fletch was talking about.

Fletch leaned back. "Come on. Nobody? Lacey, you must know what I mean."

"Not cool, Fletch," she said, her tone icy. Her features and voice lifted in delight as she dropped her hand open on the table and gathered the pot. "Y'all are totally covering my cab later, boys! So glad we've been able to get back together tonight! This has been working out well for me."

"No?"

Lacey opened her mouth to confront Fletch. Something shifted in Rob, who had put two and two together. He beat Lacey to it. "What's St. Lucia?" he asked, his tone overly innocent. He collected the cards and passed the deck to Andrew.

Fletch snorted. "Seriously. You know."

"No. Apparently not all of us do."

"All but you, you mean."

Rob looked to Andrew. Fletch's gaze bounced between them.

"Oh, come on," Fletch said, gesturing to Andrew, then Lacey. "He knows. She knows. So it's just you, Steve Carell."

"Since when did sleeping with a bartender count for such glory? Especially when I'm thinking half the city probably slept with said bartender?"

"You think she enjoyed that?" asked Lacey. Her question was fully directed at Fletch.

He shrugged. "I thought she did."

"Of course you did."

"Well. Did you have any fun? There was no 'Club Lace' to speak of."

Lacey stood, iridescent with rage and disgust. She leaned over a shrinking Fletch. "You have no idea what you're talking about. I had a grand time. At my discretion. MY discretion. I'm not sure how much of all that was truly at her discretion. Do you have any idea what I mean? Do you have any idea where the fuck she is now?"

"No," he said, more focused on his cards than he needed to be.

"Well, shut up then."

Lacey sat down. The unexpected quiet gave way to ambient sounds—the background music, the wind outside, Andrew pulling his stack of chips upward and letting them fall to the mat of the table. Clickclickclickclickclick.

"I'm in for fifty," he said, dropping the chips in the centre.

The word *fifty* resonated in their memories and collective experience, and they all smiled to differing degrees. The card game resumed. The mood almost regained its original tone of happiness and togetherness before the game dissolved a couple of hours later.

The storm had lessened some. By choice, Lacey waited for her cab on the blustery front step of Rob's bungalow. She welcomed the residual gusts that slapped her cheeks with cool ribbons of powdered snow. She didn't actually know where Lucy was now, but she knew that all places of vacation had an underbelly, their own economy, their own laws.

Charge

Aline of four-wheelers undulated over the fields and through the wooded trail. They splashed through the mud bog, creating an unbothered mess of themselves and each other. They revved in announcement of their arrival and skidded to a stop in the gravel driveway.

Lowe stepped out of the barn to greet them. Shovel in one hand, he pointed with the other to the pasture beyond. A dirty, scarred finger moved up and down in the air, tracing the location of a lone tree. "We'll bury him there," he said, his lips imperceptible under his massive beard. The riders nodded, their own beards wagging, and began to dismount.

Brian popped his head into the doorframe behind Lowe. "Hi!" he said.

The riders were still. They stared at the remarkably clean cut, buoyant young man, then at Lowe in confusion. Lowe sighed. He stood taller, his voice assertive.

"This is Brian," he said. "He's our fuckin therapist, and he lives in our basement."

Brian smiled and waved. "I'm not their therapist anymore, though."

"Whatever. Shovels in here." Lowe tilted his head. "Let's go."

Lowe's crew didn't know what to do with any of this, but they did know how to follow the instructions of their community leader, who was also by and large their employer. They filed in to grab shovels. They returned to their machines and followed Lowe and Brian, who rode a tractor floating a small front-end loader to where the procession would bury the body of Lowe's favourite, fallen horse.

Two months earlier, at mid-morning on the Thursday prior to the Easter long weekend, Lowe and Tina Sullivan plowed through the doors of Piper Valley Middle School. They bypassed the receptionist and sign-in procedures, flooding the principal's office with aggravation and anger. Red-headed twins Benny and Jenny filled two chairs with their substantial forms, boredom, and unhappiness. Fear bloomed in their faces and posture with the arrival of their parents. The principal rose from his desk, determined not to betray his own trepidation.

"This suspension bullshit has to stop. I'm fuckin done with it!" yelled Lowe.

"These kids have got just as much right as any to be here," added Tina.

Principal Wayne Fisher raised an arm in gesture, about to ask the parents to sit. He changed his mind, recalling that such a question might result in broken furniture. "They do," he said. "They also have to stop punching each other and other kids when they don't get their way—"

"Who started it this time?" Lowe hollered at his children. They rolled around in their seats and finally pointed at each other.

"—and then calling whoever steps in to prevent injury a 'useless cocksucker.'"

Tina snorted. "They're just calling a spade a spade. That's a life skill."

"They're out for two weeks. I can't risk any more injury to my teachers or students."

"Two weeks??" Lowe's face deepened another shade of red.

"Minimum."

"Can't keep making it longer and longer." Tina shook her head and looked from the twins to the principal. "What the fuck are you doing to fix it?"

Wayne opened and closed his mouth. "We've done several programs with the school counsellor, and tried to give them extra tutoring with schoolwork, and—"

"Programs!" scoffed Lowe. "Programs, my ass. That clearly ain't fixin nothing. Programs." He and Tina glanced at each other in solidarity. "Jenny's good at math and Benny's good at stories, they don't need this tutorin whatever bullshit. They're gonna lose a pile of privileges when they get home, though."

Benny and Jenny sat upright in their seats at this point. "Not again," came Benny's voice, much higher pitched than Jenny's.

"No way," Jenny said. "This is SO stupid!"

"You know what's stupid?" Lowe said, turning toward his daughter.

"It's time for ... it's time for outside supports," said Wayne, working hard to convey assertion.

The Sullivans were briefly silent. "Supports?" spat Tina. "Supports is for trussing and bras."

Benny laughed. Lowe's glare restored pallor to his son's face.

"Supports." Wayne rephrased: "Help."

This somehow resonated with Lowe. He tossed his head back. His voice carried apprehension as well as anger. "No one's takin the kids."

"No no," said Wayne, waving his hands in diffusion or reassurance, or both. The twins leaned forward in their seats, their fear tangible. Tina moved closer to them, equally troubled by the direction of things.

"I don't want that for anyone," Wayne continued. "But things are getting worse, not better, and have been since September. It's heading to that kind of phone call if something doesn't change, and soon. I'm recommending referral to a family therapist."

"Now THIS is stupid," said Tina, crossing her arms. Lowe raised his beard to the ceiling and rolled his eyes.

Wayne extended a Post-It note with some names and phone numbers. "They're all good," he said with an overtone of apology.

"What if I ain't doin this shit?" Lowe asked, volleying his glare between Wayne and the note.

"People are getting physically hurt here, Lowe. A kid and a teacher nearly went to the hospital today. This level of injury only leads to more injury. Then lawsuits, and not just for me. Your kids will only get more and more aggressive. They can't learn math or writing OR life skills like that. They can't be here right now, Lowe, because they just can't help themselves at this point. And I can't help them anymore, with things as they are." Wayne looked with concern to the children, who had resumed seventh-grade apathy in their seats, then back to their seething parents.

Lowe snatched the note. He continued to face Wayne as he yelled, "You two get in the fuckin truck. Your next two weeks are gonna be hell. NOW!" he belted. Tina pointed to the door and followed behind the twins, who gave the finger to the principal behind their heads in a wave.

"Thank you, Lowe," said Wayne, with visible relief.

"You know who's a useless cocksucker?" snapped Lowe, just before slamming the office door and stomping out after his family.

Brian T. Roth, Ph.D., silenced his Positivity Playlist by shutting his MacBook Pro. He was meeting new clients today, a family whose father had left a voicemail with a lot of swearing and a backhanded request to book an appointment. He picked up the latest copy of Wine Enthusiast and popped it in a drawer, delighted by his total agreement with their review of the Beaujolais Nouveau. As he moved the laptop to a corner of his desk, he felt a tug of anxiety related to his bank accounts, two of which were "temporarily unavailable." He closed his eyes, took a deep breath, and said to himself in a low voice, "One, two, now-on-three: all-the-po-si-ti-vi-ty!"

He and his wide smile and eyes opened his office door to the scents and sights of the Sullivans. Years of cigarette tobacco. An agitated hive of faces. "Hi!" he said. "I'm Brian. Please come in and sit where you like." He stood aside as the parade of unwashed laundry and unhappiness inundated his office. The two kids pushed back and forth a bit, and then went for the same chair. The girl got there first. The boy's manner of claiming the chair was to pick it up and dump his sister onto the floor.

"For fuck sakes!" yelled Lowe. "Benny, pick up your sister and get your ass into that other chair."

Brian continued to smile, waiting for them to settle. He sat in the remaining empty chair. They stared at him. "Start," said Lowe. "The sooner you start, the sooner this is over."

"So, I'm Brian," he said again. "Please. Introduce yourselves."

"Lowe." He then pointed to his family in sequence. "Tina, Benny, Jenny."

"Thank you. So, before we begin, I have to say a few words about confidentiality—"

Lowe was looking out the window and down to the parking lot, eyes narrowed. "You expectin anyone else?"

Brian's smile deflated slightly. "No. Why?"

"Because there's cops headin this way. Are you fuckin with us here? You call the cops on us or some fuckin social worker or somethin?"

Brian rose to see the tops of two uniformed officers and a suit. So that's what happened to my accounts. Shit.

"Shit," he said aloud, rising and grabbing his laptop and coat.

Lowe had also risen and was gesturing at the rest to get up.

"No, no," said Brian. "They're—it's not you." He stopped at the door. "Did you tell anyone you were coming here today?"

Everyone was trying to leave at once. "Fuck no," said Lowe. "You got a back door?"

Brian nodded. "Head left and take the stairs. Not the elevator."

"What did you do?" asked Lowe, as they cascaded down the back stairs to the parking garage. Brian did not respond.

In the underground parking lot, the Sullivans ran for their truck. Brian slid into his sports car, which did not start. "No." he said. "No no no no no NO NO NO"

The Sullivans were moving. The truck tires squealed as they sped past Brian.

"That man's car won't start," observed Jenny.

"Not our problem," said Lowe.

"Kind of is, Dad. He can tell them we were here."

Lowe stomped on the brakes. "Fuck me," he breathed, slamming the truck into reverse and landing back beside the sports car. He rolled down the window and yelled, "Get your ass in the back and pull the tarp over." Brian complied. Lowe slowed his exit from the garage. With no sign of the officers, who had gone in the front door and weren't anticipating a runner, Lowe sped up exponentially.

Back at the forty-seven-acre compound that was the Sullivan family home, Brian, who had absolutely no idea where he was, unrolled himself from the oil-covered tarp and lowered his bruised body from the back of the truck. "Gah," he said, his hands as messy as his suit. "This suit is a goner. EEEEEEEE" he screamed, jumping from side to side as a Doberman came barrelling and barking toward him.

Benny and Jenny howled with delight, watching Brian dance around the agitated dog in terror. "Dolly!" hollered Tina at the dog, grabbing her by the collar and leading her toward the house. "We gotta talk," she said over her shoulder to Lowe. Lowe nodded and followed. Benny and Jenny ran ahead of them into the house, leaving Brian distressed and panting in the driveway.

He was there for over an hour. It was twilight, and he was starting to get cold. He had just sat himself down on the ground with his back against the barn when Lowe and Tina came out of the house. He bounced back up as they approached.

"This is pretty fucked," said Tina, lighting a cigarette. "The last thing we wanted was to go to therapy, let alone wind up getting no shittin therapy and then having to bring you out here for goddamn some reason we don't even want to know. Is there somewhere we can take you?"

Brian had been asking himself the exact same question for the last two hours.

"So," he said, "I actually don't have anywhere to go right now."

Lowe spat a laugh and shook his head. "Bullshit."

"I'm not from here. I wasn't supposed to be here long. Also … I can't go back to my apartment just now. I can't access my car. And I have no money."

"I don't *buy* that." Tina slapped her knee with her free hand and laughed at her own pun. "You're a goddamn doctor."

"Therapist. Not a medical doctor."

"Whatever. You ain't staying here. You need fifty bucks or something?"

Brian blew air out through pursed lips. "No, really. I … my accounts have been frozen. I was running a … side business … that—"

"Hmmm," nodded Lowe. "I kinda wondered, the suit cop there with the uniform cops."

"Yeah."

"You scammin? Were we next?" Lowe moved toward Brian.

"No. No, no!" Brian held up his hands and stepped back. "Clients, never. People with too much money looking for an investment, maybe."

"Your name even Brian Roth?"

"Not sure where you want me to go," said Brian. "You've got lots of space, can I just stay here for a couple of days until I figure things out? And do you have a land line I can use?"

"I want you outta here," said Tina. "We can't trust you. And we were actually gonna trust you with family stuff."

Brian faced Tina. "Like I said, never."

The main door to the house opened, and the Doberman torpedoed toward Brian, receiving a déjà-vu reaction. Benny and Jenny were doubled over laughing in the doorway.

"You two are making things worse for yourselves by the SECOND!" screamed Tina, grabbing Dolly again and heading for the house.

Lowe watched his children's expression fade to giggling. Tina blew past them with the dog and slammed the door. When was the last time he had heard them interact with anything but screaming and fists, let alone laugh. He turned back to Brian.

"I'm gonna get you a bunch of blankets and some bread and you're on your own in the barn for the night. Don't trust you in my house. You'll make calls in the mornin and I'll drop you anywhere in a fifty-mile radius by noon."

"Okay. Whatever." Brian was shaking his head. For a therapist, whose job in part was to help people learn to problem solve by generating options, he was finding this skill to hold zero relevance for himself at the moment.

He stood motionless in the driveway as Lowe retrieved the items from the house. Lowe shoved them at Brian. "Second floor is probably cleaner. Long as it don't get too windy. It's supposed to do that tonight, I guess. If it does, then get your ass downstairs and find a corner somewhere."

"Okay."

The two men turned from each other and headed toward their separate quarters. Brian stopped and asked, "Any chance of wifi?"

"You're a lucky man right now," returned Lowe.

"Goodnight," came Brian's decreasingly cheerful voice, along with a set of lower pitched "ews" as he stepped over piles of dung. Lowe smiled despite himself.

His smile dropped as he soon as he entered the house, on his way up the stairs to remind his children that they were suspended from much more than just school, and to tell Tina that their white-collar fugitive would be gone by noon, and everything would be fine.

Except it was Lowe's truck that wouldn't start the next day. A massive oak had fallen in the night, landing on the hood and smashing a number of parts inside.

Brian stood, sleepless and cold, while Lowe swore a blue streak and paced around the truck several times.

Brian yawned. "Some irony here, I'd say," he remarked, cuddling himself.

"You didn't fuckin do this, did you? I hope for your sake you didn't."

Brian rolled his eyes and stared straight at Lowe. "Look at me, for Christ's sake."

Lowe kicked the runner. "Fuck this. You ain't stayin here. Come on." He marched to the barn and over to one of the four-wheelers, Brian following cautiously behind. Lowe started it up and got on. "Get on the back."

"It's freezing. How far are we going?"

"As far as wherever I'm droppin you."

"I have nowhere to go. I told you." Brian had, in fact, made no calls, because there was no one to call.

"You are NOT MY FUCKIN PROBLEM!" yelled Lowe. Jesus, thought Brian, it's 8:30 a.m., so much yelling and swearing, no cappuccino for coping. "Get the fuck on here. I'll leave you at the highway truck stop, if nothin else. NOW."

Brian carefully mounted the vehicle. "Seriously, nowhere. No one. No money."

"Tina made me take fifty bucks to give you."

"Great. Thanks. Where are the helmets?"

Lowe tore out of the barn. Brian screamed and clutched onto him for dear life as they flew over the hills.

Two hours later, Tina had physically separated Benny and Jenny for the fifth time, and was running out of things to threaten to take away from them. She had just sat back down at the kitchen table and was lighting a cigarette when she heard the four-wheeler skid into the driveway and then Lowe's voice, angrier than usual. He was hollering at someone. The voice got louder, the door opened, and Lowe stomped into the kitchen.

"Trees down everywhere. EVERYWHERE. I can't get him outta here. Roads closed. Trails blocked. Could go through the river, but it's too fuckin cold. I don't want this asshole here!"

"Fuck sakes," echoed Tina. Dolly had woken up from a nap and trotted over to greet Lowe. Lowe turned and raised his hand, but held it when Tina asked, "So, what'd you do with him?"

"Fuck him. I'm off to the pit." He stomped back out the door. The four-wheeler started up again and roared away.

Silence grew, inside and out. The kids must have gone back to sleep; it was their way of passing the time when punished. They were quite good at it, but never during hours that were convenient for their mother. She butted out her cigarette and went outside. She found Brian sitting once again with his back to the barn door, this time with his arms wrapped around his knees, shaking with cold. His breathing was audible from a distance. She walked over to him.

"I don't have time for you," she said. "But what I really don't have time for is you getting pneumonia or some damn thing and then trying to find you a doctor or you dying on us or some shit like that. He'll be pissed, but we're putting you in the basement for a day or two until our truck gets fixed. That's it. Then he'll drop your ass at the relay." She took a handful of dog treats out of her pocket and handed them to Brian. "You're gonna need these."

Stiff from cold and his night on the barn floor, Brian pulled himself up and reached for the treats. "You make these yourself?" he asked through his chattering teeth, rolling the odd shapes around in his hand.

"Mmm-hmm. From the livers of the last run of rabbits we snared." She started to walk. "You'll stay down there, by the way. Meals, everything. You set foot upstairs, Dolly'll let us know—and she'll let you know, too."

Brian now felt nausea along with the deep cold in his gut. His options had expanded ever so slightly, from none to terrible. He put one foot in front of the other. Maybe a solution would come to him by the time the truck was fixed.

Tina opened the door, Dolly lost her mind, and Brian tried not to lose his.

Down in the damp, unfinished basement, Brian found himself surrounded by decades of disorganized piles of furniture with boxes upon boxes heaped on top. He wasn't habituating to the smell or to the inadequate light of the one swinging bulb. After a while, the door at the top of the stairs opened. No one descended. Instead, a bed roll was fired down the stairs. He jumped out of the way. The bed roll was followed by a filthy bucket and toilet paper, some blankets, and a pillow of some sort. A sports team-sized thermos thudded down the stairs, followed by some clothing and another loaf of bread. Silence. A battered magazine fluttered partway down. Brian approached. Playboy, 1987.

At the top of the stairs, Benny and Jenny giggled, and slammed the door.

"Thanks!" called Brian cheerfully. He had perfected cheer. He heard it ring clear in his voice, the discord remarkable against the ache and dismay he felt in every cell of his body.

His cell phone indicated 114 new emails. He cringed as he powered it down. He had no charger, and being located wasn't any more in his best interest than his current mess was.

Inching himself into the overalls and work shirt that he had received, he found himself unfathomably close to the family's smell, and to Lowe's in particular. He choked a bit, trying not to gag. He ignored the sketchy bed roll and pushed the contents of a couch to the floor. He wrapped himself in the blankets, regrettably laid his head on the stained pillow, and fell into a profound sleep.

✳

The sound of a dog losing its mind beside his ear sent Brian into high alert. He opened his eyes to a close-up of Dolly's teeth, and screamed. He leapt up onto the back of the couch, his heart slamming in his chest.

"Get up here, you're leaving!" hollered Lowe over the barking, from the top of the stairs.

"I … can't move." panted Brian, this being a true statement. Dolly wouldn't give him an inch.

"Dolly!" bellowed Lowe. Dolly slinked off and up the stairs. Then there were sounds of furniture scraping, the dog whimpering, and a slammed door.

Brian changed back into his semi-dried, oil-stained, barn-scented suit, preparing himself as best he could. He shrugged in surrender and climbed the stairs.

In the kitchen, Benny sat staring blankly at a math book. He spun a small hunting knife around and around on the table. Brian saw that the boy's right index finger was badly scarred. He stifled the instinct to ask about it. The dog was nowhere to be seen. Lowe stood against the stove, red-faced and downing the last of his coffee.

"Math is stupid," said Benny, shoving the book away.

"You're stupid," said his father.

Brian stifled a cringe.

"Not doing it."

"What?" asked Tina, entering the kitchen with a crate of eggs.

"Not doing math. They don't want me back in school, so I don't care. Don't care about math. Don't care what you do about it anymore. To me." Benny crossed his arms and sat back in his chair.

Shit, thought Brian.

Lowe threw his coffee mug across the room. He picked up Benny with one fist and punched him in the face with the other. He dropped Benny back into his seat. Benny slumped over, gasping, covering his nose. Tina put the eggs on the counter. She shook her head and picked up a dishtowel. "God I hate this," she said, looking sideways at Lowe, who had retreated back to the stove to glare at his son. She opened the freezer, wrapped a bag of peas in the towel, and handed it to Benny.

"I fuckin hate you," muttered Benny.

"What was that?" asked Lowe.

Benny stiffened, sensing his mistake and a much greater level of trouble.

Lowe launched back toward Benny. He found himself running into Brian, who had stepped between the two. Lowe slapped both of his giant palms onto Brian's chest and shoved him sideways. Brian righted himself and leapt back between them. In response, Lowe grabbed Brian by the hair on the top of his head with one hand and his clothing with the other and threw him aside. Brian winced, steadied himself, and shot back into the fray again.

"Not your fuckin issue!" spat Lowe.

"No, it's a goddamn Child Protection issue, except I can't call them!" returned Brian.

Lowe, Tina, and Benny's faces registered shock, but Lowe's was brief. He swung for Brian, who ducked. Lowe came after him and slammed him onto the table.

Jenny had appeared in the doorway. "Dad, don't," she said, her voice all but a whisper.

Tina had hustled Benny over to the doorway and was now yelling at both kids to get upstairs. They stood frozen against each other. She moved back toward the fight, yelling, "Lowe, quit it!"

Brian was trying to rise from the table as Lowe reached for him. He slithered out from Lowe's grip and tried to upend him from the knees. Lowe laughed between grunts. "Fuckin useless," he ground out between his teeth. He kneed Brian in the nose. Brian bucked and wobbled backward. Just as Lowe swung, Brian kicked his knees, throwing him off balance. The full force of Lowe's fist collided with Tina's jaw. She yowled and dropped to her hands and knees, blood beginning to pour from her mouth.

"Fuck!" said Lowe. "Fuck. Fuck fuck fuck." He approached his wife, who raised her palm for him to stop. He stepped back, his eyes wide. He landed in a kitchen chair.

A dense period of silence followed, permeated by the heavy breathing of three dishevelled adults and two terrified children.

Tina finally sat back on her knees. She was still unable to catch her breath. "This is too much," she wheezed. "It's a shitshow the likes of which I never wanted. I never wanted this." She began to cry. "This can't go on, Lowe. I can't do it."

Lowe turned to Brian. "You start tomorrow."

"Start what?" asked Brian. He patted his cut cheek and grimaced at the sight of blood on his already filthy hand.

"What we went to you for in the fuckin first place. I never hit my wife before—well, once, a long fuckin time ago. I haven't done it since. Hadn't," he corrected himself. "Fuck. So now if this means we all gotta go to fuckin therapy, so be it." He turned his face to the window. His voice was quieter, approaching sadness. "Looks like we don't know much what else to do, besides hittin."

Brian felt himself fill with panic. "But I found a place to go—"

"You said you don't take advantage of people like us. So don't start lyin now. You start tomorrow. We—" he looked at the disarray of his family— "start tomorrow."

"But I need to—"

"Never mind what you fuckin need. We'll get you a better bed. You can come up for meals. Just shut the fuck up for now. You start talkin tomorrow."

Brian shook his head in disbelief and denial. This wasn't happening. He felt distorted, everything felt distorted. He exhaled long and deep, buying some time to think. It dawned on him that he might have some bargaining power. "May I have a shower?"

"What part about tomorrow don't you get?" Lowe pointed to the basement door.

An hour later, the basement door opened. Down smashed another large thermos of water, followed by a wad of clean-ish towels, and a mostly used bar of soap. Brian ran to pick up the soap. He held it to his nose and inhaled the scent of Irish Spring, the soap he grew up with. The long-ago, cellular memory of family comfort exploded in his chest, and he sobbed and sobbed.

The Sullivan family treatment plan was immersive and comprehensive in a way that Brian had never anticipated designing or applying, let alone living. There was individual and family work, although Lowe refused to participate in the one-to-one sessions or in meditation. This became an increasing bone of contention with Tina. The unorthodox inpatient/ day program was not without its flaws and setbacks. Following a second incident of family violence, although its consequences were not as terrible, Brian retreated deliberately to the basement. This time, he did so with Dolly, a fresh bag of rabbit liver treats, and a lot of talking himself through his own fear. He announced loudly that he was cancelling therapy for two days.

It was at Benny and Jenny's insistence at the end of the first day that therapy resumed. They made their case at the top of the stairs, pointing clumsily at their feelings list while lightly shoving one another. Brian noted that their constant jostling now had a hint of affection to it. They were returning to school soon and didn't feel ready. Their fledgeling attempts to convey this were misphrased and awkward, but definitely in line with the work they had been doing, and so Brian wordlessly climbed the stairs. Dolly stayed in the basement, where it was her turn to sleep soundly for a long period of time.

Brian learned that Benny could draw quite well. One of his tasks had been to re-create, with imagery, the feelings list that Brian had convinced Tina to download and print from the internet. Benny's work had been surprisingly well laid out. They worked on changes to his versions of the facial expressions, and he learned to draw a range beyond anger and discomfort.

Brian suspected that Jenny was a natural introvert in a family configuration where volume and force were the status quo for most interactions. She likely hadn't experienced much encouragement in the realm of expressing emotions and needs through language. Her feelings list was more word based, with the prompt to choose colourful fonts and add fun images. Sometimes this was with the help of her brother, who subsequently adopted a portion of the new lexicon.

For each finished piece of therapy "homework," Brian would act out Lowe's favourite horse, Barnaby, doing ridiculous things. Barnaby at a disco, Barnaby the Barista, Barnaby on the Olympic curling team. The kids' homework completion time shrunk from never to same-day.

Brian discovered that the farm had belonged to Tina's family—her grandparents had been affluent. Her parents started out on a similar track before an accident in the fields killed her mother shortly after the birth of Tina's youngest brother. Her father never emotionally recovered, and the money vaporized. Tina had essentially raised herself and three younger siblings. As to the contemporary "family business," Tina would not speak in particulars, and Brian didn't dream of asking Lowe. Brian had caught the occasional glimpse of the Sullivan's IT setup, contemporary in contrast to the rest of their lodgings and appliances. It was also excruciatingly inaccessible, in a room beyond a steel door with two deadbolts.

Lowe refused to speak to Brian at all except in the form of orders, although the orders were accompanied by a slight decrease in swearing. Brian quietly began to express orders of his own. A bathroom of sorts had been installed in the basement, as well as a reading lamp, by which he spent his evenings with the antiquated periodicals and newspapers he came by in boxes among long forgotten family heirlooms. The year 1953 was more interesting than he had ever thought to imagine.

Occasionally, Brian heard what he thought were explosions. He found this puzzling, but chalked it up to trucks backfiring on the distant highway or to the constant messing around of four-wheelers in the woods and fields. Something to do with engine-y things, anyway.

On the morning the Sullivan twins were to return to school, Principal Wayne stood at the window of his office. He tried not to hyperventilate as the Sullivan's truck pulled up, on time, in front of the school. Benny and Jenny spilled out and lumbered toward the building, coats undone, boots half off. Lowe followed up the rear on his own, as Tina's cuts and the bruising to her face had not yet healed enough for her to be seen. Other than Tina's absence, nothing looked different to Wayne. He sighed.

"Welcome back, Benny and Jenny," said Wayne with an animated smile and a silent prayer that he appeared sincere.

"Yeah okay," said Jenny. "Hi!" said Benny brightly.

Wayne was dumbfounded as they marched past him through the front door. They had never addressed him before. "So, did they see the therapist?" he asked Lowe.

"Fuckin pile of work and money," shot Lowe. "Long way to go still."

"Hmmm," said Wayne, still in shock. "That's good start, though! Whoever you called seems to have done a lot in two weeks. That Roth one, though, apparently he's gone AWOL due to involvement in some sort of financial scam. So sorry I put a criminal on that list I gave you, Lowe, I had NO idea. Thank God you didn't call him." Meanwhile, Lowe had begun to walk away. "Let's talk about the plan going forward, I've—"

"No plan," came Lowe's voice as he continued out the front door. "You do your part and keep them here this time."

"We still need to establish a safety—"

The truck door slammed. Lowe's opinion on the matter was expressed through enhanced air and noise pollution as he powered out of the parking lot.

Upon return to the compound, Lowe went to tend to Barnaby, who seemed to Brian to be Lowe's only overt object of affection. In the barn, Lowe found not only his horse, but Brian.

"What the fuck are you doin here?" asked Lowe.

"Hi!" said Brian.

"I'm not talkin to you. This is a fuckin ambush, this. Get the fuck out."

Brian shook his head. "Nope. No ambush. Besides, I'm done for the day. I … was hoping I could learn how to ride."

Lowe snorted. "You couldn't ride a Ferris wheel. And no. This ain't the horse for you." He snickered a bit and inclined his head toward the horse in the next stall. "You might try Troy there." Troy looked quite affable, and as though he subsisted on cheeseburgers instead of hay. Lowe's facial expression turned to puzzlement. "So why you seriously out here, now?"

"City boy. Once in a lifetime opportunity to branch out, you know. In so many ways. For sooo many things." Brian raised his eyebrows and sighed.

"You guys have tried many new things. Maybe I want to try something new, too. Like, of my own volition?"

Lowe paused. He found this a reasonable argument but wasn't about to concede. "Nope. Now get outta here. This is my time away from everybody. Including you."

Brian took his time removing himself from the barn, pausing in the doorway. Barnaby's head followed his every move. He continued to stare at the empty doorframe after Brian left.

"Barn. Barnaby. Over here, now," whispered Lowe, seeking the attention of his friend. Barnaby remained fixated on the absent man.

Lowe put his face in his palms. "Jesus, Jesus, Jesus, JESUS." He dropped his hands and yelled, "Come back here, asshole!"

"Brian," said Brian, popping his head in. "That is how we address me, as we agreed."

"For fuck sakes. B, Br, Brraaaaaghhhhhh. Tomorrow, we'll revisit this stupid idea tomorrow."

"Is it a stupid idea? Or just an idea?" Lowe's breathing changed in a way Brian recognized readily. "Goodnight!" he waved, backing out of the doorway.

On their first ride, embodied by ease and flow for Lowe and Barnaby and all kinds of bouncy awkwardness for Brian and Troy, Lowe lead them to a giant pit. Brian was floored by the depth and scope of it. "Whoa," he said. "What happened here?"

"Fire in the hole!" came a cracked, pubescent voice, followed by a massive explosion that caused Brian to scream and duck under Troy's substantial neck, covering the back of his head with his hands.

Gravel dropped within a few feet of them. Dust rose everywhere, eclipsing the entirety of the pit and landscape. The horses weren't bothered. Brian couldn't breathe for shock; Lowe couldn't breathe for laughing at Brian's reaction. As the dust dissipated, Benny emerged from behind a nearby tree with a remote control device of some sort. "Good one!" said Lowe.

"I made the adjustments like you said."

"Good. Try to get more range, now," said Lowe, gesturing with his hands to indicate a greater distance. Brian's eyes were drawn to Lowe's hands and their scarred fingers, identical to his son's. The process was not without trial and error. Jesus, he said under his breath.

Benny, puffed up with pleasure at his explosion and his father's rare praise, nodded to himself over and over as he opened the doors to a bunker. He descended, a pudgy arm guiding the horizontal doors shut above him. Lowe caught Brian's eye and gestured, by tilting his head, for Brian to sit up. Brian realized that he was still parallel and clinging to Troy's neck.

"So this is …" began Brian, straightening up.

"Part of our industry," finished Lowe. "Boy is getting better. He'll need to take over here someday. He's not smart like Jenny."

Brian suppressed disagreement. "So this is … your family business?"

"It's a part of our business." Lowe turned to face Brian. "Business. You know the ins and outs of business, don't you, Bry-yan?"

Brian was unsure as to where this line of dialogue might lead. He steered it toward the scene at hand. "The horses—"

"Trained to handle the sound. They know the warning call. Now you do, too."

"Umm-hmmm," vocalized Brian, wondering why he couldn't have pleasantly learned to ride a horse while on his séjour here in the middle of nowhere without exposure to even more Sullivan extreme family weirdness. His heartbeat was beginning to approach a normal rate when Lowe said, "Shit. Shit! Come on!" Lowe hauled on Barnaby's reins and shouted at Troy in a way that sent Troy flying, as best as Troy could, behind Barnaby, reeling one hundred and eighty degrees and charging back toward the barn.

"What the hell?!" screamed Brian as the horse and his body slammed along the uneven ground. So much screaming today.

Lowe said nothing and raced on. Brian, terrified of many things, risked a quick glance behind him. Beyond the dust and the far side of the pit, he saw a tiny group of four-wheelers moving in their direction. Lowe didn't want to be seen. More accurately, Brian surmised, Lowe didn't want Brian to be seen.

"Get off. Basement," ordered Lowe as they reached the house. He leapt from Barnaby, grabbing the reins of both horses. Brian unintuitively slid down the side of the horse and landed in a pile on the ground. "NOW, FUCKER!" Lowe hollered, with more urgency than disgust. "If any of them see you, I don't know who's gonna get killed, you or me. Get the fuck outta here!" He positioned the horses to block any view of Brian going into the house, and Brian scurried down to the basement.

Why am I doing this, again? he thought. He dropped down onto the couch, working to catch his breath. The house door opened and shut, over and over. Boisterous voices, swearing, and stomping filled the air above him. There was the sound of fridge opening and bottle caps pinging against the stove, the floor, the walls. The light grew dim in the basement windows as the volume increased upstairs. At one point, Lowe opened the basement door briefly and flung a sandwich that deconstructed itself on the way down.

The party carried on until the windows turned light with dawn. Where is Tina, where are the kids, Brian thought at one point. He never heard their voices. He slept superficially, out of vigilance, all the while aware that they weren't around. And what would he have done, anyway. He recalled the race to the house and his deposition; Lowe wasn't into having his friends meet his family therapist-in-residence. Lowe wasn't into family therapy at all, and clearly he did not think his friends would approve. Or maybe they'd think Lowe was gay, or Brian was a narc, or any combination of things. Regardless, based on today's revelations, Brian had come to a heightened realization that he had no idea what sort of world he was currently living in.

It's time to go, he thought. In his waking moments throughout the long noisy night, he planned how to prepare the family for his quickest possible exit. Something Lowe couldn't argue with. Something he could walk away from, morally. Somewhere to walk to.

Brian applied the last bit of colour to the third whiteboard with a flourish. He spun to Tina, Benny, and Jenny with a well-practiced dance move.

"Evaluation?" asked Jenny, reading the last word he had written.

"Like a test?" asked Benny.

"No tests," said Tina.

"Not a test," he laughed. "It's like a last check-in. You know, like we do every day and then every week, but this time, we check in over the whoooole—" he gestured over a hand-drawn, six-week calendar of days and colour-coded activities "—thing. You did it! You've completed the program!"

The twins' faces projected a mix of surprise and sadness. Tina seemed surprised and uncertain in equal measure.

"And you get to evaluate … me!"

Benny and Jenny smiled a little. "I like that idea," said Jenny.

"Does Lowe know about this?" asked Tina.

"No. Where is he, anyway? He knows we start on time." Brian turned back to his whiteboards, exercising all manner of will to contain his glee at the tangibly imminent conclusion of this exceptionally bizarre chapter of his life. "Where are your workbooks?" His question was directed to Benny and Jenny, who had arrived at the session empty handed. They skipped out of the room and raced up the stairs.

Tina looked over the whiteboards. "Can't believe you put 'teach breathing exercise' on there. Kids were born knowing how to breathe."

"Exactly," he said, drawing a joyful check mark next to that item.

"So where are you going then?" Tina suddenly couldn't look at Brian. She crushed an imaginary cigarette with the ball of her shoe, something he had seen Jenny do a thousand times.

"I've got a plan. I just need a proper shower, and my suit back." He cringed. "Oh yeah. I may need to ask for you to get the suit dry cleaned."

"That makes no sense. Dry cleaned? What, you take some alcohol and a hair dryer to it?"

Brian bit his lips, unsure how to explain inoffensively that he needed a suit that appeared, as much as possible, as though it hadn't been dipped in engine oil and used as a horse barn stall mat. "Just maybe let me borrow your washer, just the once? It needs a delicate cycle, if I can't get it to a dry cleaner."

"You need a delicate cycle." Her mouth remained tight, but her eyes twinkled.

He allowed himself a smile in return. He had overheard her being quite funny with the men who came by, but she had never engaged in humour with him.

"Why, Tina," he said, "put a good word for me in your evaluation. I got something right if I managed a joke out of you."

"I'm not evaluating a fucking thing. Go get your fancy pants."

Down in the basement, Brian climbed over furniture and objects to a corner space where he had hung his suit six weeks earlier. It was familiar yet tragic, its beautiful tailoring and its stains that were likely past hope. He had daydreamed obsessively about steaming his suit while he had a very hot shower, followed by much delicate spot scrubbing, a couple of light runs through the washer, and a day on the line in the sun. And the shoes …. Brian looked down to where Prada had taken a great fall. "I'm sorry," he whispered, bending down to pick up his mud-caked derbies. He recalled their last day above ground: his office, checking his calendar, his frozen bank accounts, all in complete denial of his arrogance. He remembered covering himself in the back of the truck with the slimy and mud-caked tarp, inhaling fumes for the duration of the ride. He remembered stepping in horse dung in the darkness and curling himself into an aching ball next to Barnaby, who moved closer to him in the storm, somehow aware that he needed the heat. What a ride. What a fuckin ride.

A ruckus banged into effect upstairs. The door slammed open, Lowe's footfalls faster and heavier across the house than usual. There was a low whine, unbearably human. Rapid footfalls pounded toward the door. "Lowe? Lowe, don't," came Tina's voice, increasing in fear and volume. "LOWE, DON'T!"

Brian launched up the stairs. Tina paced in the kitchen, tears streaming down her face. "He's got the gun," she howled, "and he's upset, he's so upset, he's so sad for so long, I don't know what he's gonna do, I don't know what to——"

A four-wheeler started up and revved away.

"I'll stay with the kids," said Brian. "You go after him, Tina, he loves you, he won't—"

"It's not me. I'm not worried about me—it's him."

Brian ran from the house toward the barn. It had been a dry start to the summer and a dust cloud hung, drawing a path where the four-wheeler had been. He ran into the barn and looked at Troy. Nope. He spun around. His eyes landed on the other four-wheelers, with no idea how to even start them up. "Fuuuuck fuck fuck fuck," he said over and over, standing by one of the machines and trying to remember what the family always did to get them revving. He got on, pressed and turned a series of things, and jolted when it started. He got the four-wheeler moving jerkily out of the barn, made a mess of shifting gears, and gathered some degree of control. He increased speed in pursuit of Lowe.

Fear began to expand from his insides. What do I do when I find him? What will I even find? Who will I even find?

The trail of dust ended at the edge of the pit. Lowe was all but collapsed against the same tree where Benny had stood a couple of weeks earlier with his explosives rig. The pit had expanded hideously, the edge of the ground eroded and raw. Lowe's feet dangled over its edge. One hand lay on the shotgun, parallel to his legs, the other tightly gripped a 40-ouncer of whiskey. His breathing was hard and mechanical, his eyes low, trance-like. Brian's heart raced. His instinct was to rush to the man, but the man had a gun and a poor grip on self-control.

Brian slowly approached the scene, not knowing if Lowe was even aware of him. He delicately stepped toward the new edge of the pit, scarred like the hands of father and son, and looked down. "Oh," he breathed, his voice shaking.

Barnaby lay several feet down. The ground was angled enough to provide a bit of a shelf on which his body was cradled. His front legs were at different angles altogether. Brian's breakfast launched into his throat, but he managed to stop it there. His shock rolled into despair as he saw the horse was still alive.

"I can't, I can't," came Lowe's voice. It was as odd and broken as Barnaby's legs. In slow motion, Lowe let go of the bottle and picked up the gun. Brian jumped back. "I can't—" Lowe pointed the gun down toward the pit, where he had a clear shot. "I can't." Unable to pull the trigger, he started to lower the gun back to the ground. "I can't." Brian felt the slightest sense of relief. Then Lowe clumsily reached for the gun again and began to turn it toward himself.

Brian was able to move faster than the heavily drunken Lowe. He grabbed the gun, jamming his foot into Lowe's shoulder for extra force. Lowe growled through his sobs and began to push himself up from the ground in Brian's direction. Brian turned to the pit. His arms quaked as he aimed the gun at the horse and hollered, "DON'T THINK DON'T THINK DON'T THINK DON'T" and pulled the trigger.

Barnaby's form stopped rising and falling. Brian dropped the gun. He staggered sideways and fell to the ground, his own legs unable to carry him. The shock of firing the gun and killing the animal began to flood his system, and he rocked back and forth. Only at the last minute did he see Lowe lunging for the gun, and that it was double-barrelled. Brian dove for the gun and fired the last bullet into the air. He flung the gun into the pit.

At this point he doubled over, fully sick. Leaning back into a sitting posture, he spat repeatedly and saw Lowe collapsed into the tree. He appeared to be in a drunken sleep.

Brian crawled over to grab the bottle of whiskey. He sank what was left of it, hoping for any degree of stupor, which didn't turn out to be much. He backed away, sitting a few feet from Lowe and waiting for his own system to settle in any way. At all. Waiting. Waiting.

His senses registered the sound of an approaching four-wheeler. It stopped. He turned slowly to see Tina and a man dismounting. Tina was tentative in her steps, shaken. Brian nodded as if to say, he's okay. Tina and the man looked around, piecing together what had happened, and then Tina knelt beside Lowe. Brian raised himself up and walked back to the house, which took an indefinable amount of time. Since his arrival on the farm, time had gradually lost meaning. At this moment, it truly had no meaning at all.

He was unable to reconcile the day. He was unable to reconcile the last few months, or the whole of his existence. There was no boundary to the reeling of his head and guts, this unprecedented level of agitation and exhaustion, and the clarity and depth of the stars that had begun to emerge in the giant country sky. The final and brightest star was that of an outdoor light on the house, which flooded the yard and the side of the barn. Brian entered the barn and, as if on autopilot, headed to the corner near Barnaby's stall where he had spent his first night. He lay down in a ball, his whole body consumed by the vibrating of his hands from the recoil of the gun, and the recoil of his world.

A voice sounding remotely like Lowe's called Brian's name. Brian opened his eyes and looked around the basement, as if seeing these surroundings for the first time. He had no recollection of getting there. He mentally grasped at the objects around him, trying to render them familiar.

The voice called again. Gentle. A subdued Lowe? Someone related to him?

Brian staggered as he got up and put one foot in front of the other on the stairs. Seeing his hands, he realized someone had washed them; his fingernails were cut short and fine for the first time in months. He was arrested in absurdity. The hands he saw were familiar to him, yet he floated above them, wondering how they were his.

A woman emerged from the bathroom, freshly showered, her long body wrapped in one Frette bath towel and her hair in another. She smiled and walked over to her newest lover. She wrapped her arms around him from behind as he poured hot water into a French press. "Hello."

"Hi!" he said, leaning back into her.

She shifted to see around him. The wall was a line of ceiling-to-floor windows framing a phenomenal skyline view of the city and the lake beyond. The hundreds of distant rectangular silos that made up the down-town core were dark, backlit by the early morning sun.

"Your place is beautiful, Paul." She righted herself, placing her nose on his showered neck. "Your soap, though! Irish Spring? So retro. What's up with that?"

His hand descended deliberately with the coffee plunger, his eyes following the tiny air bubbles as they rose along the inside of the glass. "Reminds me of home."

Hotelier

I started my first job at the Ash-Ronson Mountain Resort in 1994. It was an exorbitant, movie set-like operation on a lake in the mountains, with its own runway, helicopter fleet, and private beach, as well as access to a second private beach for an inconceivable fee. The view of the mountains and the lake was astonishing from every angle. You would expect to feel a divide between the types of people who came to stay. There were those who had more money than even the one percent could fathom, and there were those who had made this stay a life goal and had exercised and amassed all possible means to get there. Yet there was no divide. An Ash-Ronson guest was an Ash-Ronson guest.

The staff was another manner of tapestry altogether. I met rich kids whose parents had forced them to get jobs, and I met young parents barely feeding their kids. Some people thought they were awesome, some barely clung to reality. Others did both. Everyone had to submit criminal record checks, but that didn't mean much. The larger-than-life characters were offset by silent shadows in uniform who blended into the back hallways. You didn't perceive them if they stood still. Some had arrived on planes or even boats from overseas, never having met their families. There was a great great niece of Jane Fonda's. I lost count of the countries and situations people hailed from.

I wasn't sure where Pan Jon Hawthorne fit. In 1996, I estimated his age at somewhere between 55 and 70 years old. He had been working the front desk since 1965. He carried himself with the slightest stoop within his already moderate 5-foot-6 elevation. His height was transcended by the tidal force of character that exuded from and around him as he commanded a front desk the length of a football field. He was relatively quiet, given his position and reputation, yet you knew he was in a room before you saw him. Then came the signature visuals: the raging pencil moustache dyed to match his hair, the incredible neck scarves, the raw yet gentle energy in his hazel eyes. He resonated with older celebrities and younger influencers both. He was familiar to me before I came to the hotel, on account of the incidental passage of his images in magazines—*Chatelaine, MacLean's*.

We didn't see Pan outside of the formalities of work. From my initial station, I barely saw him at all. Over the three summers I worked there, I moved from laundry to kitchen and, finally, to room service night delivery. There wasn't much occasion to be in the lobby, especially during the day. I spotted him in attendance, as a guest, at a couple of celebrity weddings when I was brought in as a banquet server. There, his scarves burst into full-blown suits of Italian design and Indian flare, with shoes that had been altered to match, all animated to even higher visual heights by his effervescent personality and flawless ballroom dancing. The beautifully controlled movement of his body defied any of my estimates of his age. He was the happening of every happening.

He once made an unusual appearance in the staff cafeteria. It was seamless. He moved effortlessly and without people fawning all over him, which took me everything not to do. He leaned over to one of his front desk colleagues, talking of how he so enjoyed the guest chef's prosciutto vols-au-vent and wanted to savour them in the company of his colleagues, knowing they would enjoy them just as much. He was right about the vols-au-vent; I was smitten. Smitten with the food, smitten with the opulence of five-star hotel functioning, smitten with this man and how he somehow brought so many different people and scenes together while being entirely himself.

I returned my tray and exited the cafeteria through the service hallway in the direction of the conference centre. There was an awards event that evening around which the planners had been more piqued and ill-tempered than usual. I felt myself puffing up prior to returning, so as to deliver the proper mix of servitude and confidence. In the hallway, Pan and a man about half his age were speaking quietly and close together. It was the guest chef. Awkwardness flared in my cheeks and gut. I got a grip on myself, lowered my head, and moved to pass.

Pan turned from his conversation to me. He was the full technicolour force of everything I knew of him from a distance. He inclined his head, a demand formed as a request for me to stop. I stopped.

"Your hair, my dear," he said, not looking at my hair but straight into my eyes like he had known me forever. "Humour yourself, and me, and layer it. Feather it within an inch of its velvet life. Colour it dark in the front, light through the rest. Get a suit fitted to that gorgeous body of yours. You won't look back."

Neither did he. He resumed his intimate conversation. I carried his comments with me into the fray of the evening and the party, the after-party, the after-party's after-party, and far beyond. I left the Ash-Ronson in the late fall of 1998, enrolled in hospitality school, and worked my way back ten years later.

This time, I started my job by walking through the front doors, three bell staff in tow wrangling boxes, suitcases, and garment bags. It was a massive task to contain my joy at entering the lobby. I channelled the poise and mien of the management I had become. I engaged in a series of compulsory greetings and was guided around the front desk to my new office.

I was present, pleasant, and pleased, all the while keeping an eye out for Pan. I had been waiting to see him, to talk to him, to meet him as a peer. This underlying dream and intention had guided me away from the hotel and back again, through so many decisions and crazy experiences leading up to this moment.

I asked the general manager about him. "He's around," he smiled. This was all that was said. He was indeed around; he made an appearance two days later, greeting guests and checking them in.

Time had tried to stand still, but did not quite. The stoop was noticeable, the internal glow just as wondrous but shorter in range. His face was more sallow. The hair dye had not changed a shade on his head or his pencil moustache, and his laugh was unaltered. Upon hearing it, I was nineteen again, smelling of cleaning product in my housekeeping uniform instead of perfume in my present-day Saks Fifth Avenue skirt and jacket. This felt equally comforting and disorienting.

I carried through to my office. I did not manage to speak with him that day, or even that week. The blur of the new position was unfathomable in its demand, exhaustion, and excitement.

On an early evening in May, when the sun was starting to show true promise of summer, I saw Pan donning his overcoat in the office off the front desk. He had concluded whatever shift he had been working. His shifts were irregular in timing and duration. I dropped what I was doing, and approached.

"Pan, I'm Leigh. I'm so pleased to meet you. I'm the new Event Services Executive Officer. I wanted to make sure to say hello."

"Yes, I know. And welcome." He smiled his front-page smile and righted his shirtsleeves within his coat.

I tried not to be tentative. I succeeded in appearance, if not in feeling. "Might you be willing to have a drink with me sometime?"

"Yes, indeed. You'll follow me?"

I didn't see this coming. "Absolutely. One moment as I fetch my coat."

I followed him through the back hallways and tunnels and eventually up the stairs to an exit. As we made our way, Pan talked of everything and nothing—the weather, the guests, last month's scandal involving royalty and DJs that should have been costly but turned profitable. We walked a short path to a set of low-rise buildings opposite the grounds maintenance area. Each building was a roadside motel that had been transported to the property. They had received little structural upkeep beyond repeated coatings of white paint. We stopped at a door, which he opened from a bulky key ring. I hadn't opened a door with a metal key in years.

Two motel rooms had been combined into a single unit, crammed ceiling-to-floor with paraphernalia and curio spanning decades. Wildly designed lamps, art deco posters of what would have been racy bars and dance clubs in their era, restaurant and hotel signage in various Eastern European and Asian languages, collections of figurines. One corner had been done up as a department store window display with several mannequins wearing spectacular suits, some of which I remembered Pan wearing. Other mannequins wore equally opulent and outrageous dresses. One of the lamps looked exactly like the leg lamp from *A Christmas Story*, and it occurred to me that it might well be the actual lamp. Opposite the clothing, a mirror loomed with the title PanAm across the top and the misogyny of 'Smile? Posture? Makeup? Weight?' down the side.

Pan sized me up. "Plymouth? Belvedere?" he asked, proceeding to mix martinis without waiting for a response. The cocktail shaker vibrated in one hand as he moved to re-open the door with the other. "Warm for this time of year, isn't it? Especially for here, in the mountains. Please," he gestured toward the furniture in the tiny square footage that constituted his living room.

We sat kitty-corner in high-backed chairs that came from a previous incarnation of the Ash-Ronson's lobby. My view now was of the open door, framing the magnificence of the mountains in the background and a maintenance shed in the foreground. A barbed-wire fence guarded tractors and Gator utility vehicles. A pile of broken industrial washers unworthy of protection sat outside of the fencing.

Everything was otherworldly, including the martini. "Brilliant," I said.

"My favourite as well. So from where do you join us?"

I couldn't help myself. "Do you remember me?"

"Oh darling, of course I do." He had turned toward me in his seat. I was now the object of all the attention and familiarity he had perfected over a lifetime of guest service and tens of thousands of superficial interactions.

"You're one of us."

He had no idea who I was.

The sun set over a second martini, a silver plate of leftover hors-d'oeuvres, and a walk-through of the hospitality awards and photos that covered one entire wall. Sensing the end of the interaction, I rose and thanked him. He would have no clue how overwhelmed I was by everything I had taken in, the flood of pictures in my mind and heart. The suits, the awards, the piles of gravel and appliances, the view of the mountains beyond. My bravado and excitement had been supplanted by a jangly mix of pleasure, sadness, and discomfort.

I breathed as much of the clean mountain air as my lungs could stand as I walked back to the main hotel, where my contemporary 25th floor lodging awaited. Con-temporary, I thought. How temporary? How con?

I took my time with each step, wondering if I would ever retrace them.

The Lighthouse

The lighthouse came into view around the corner of the cliff face. It disappeared and re-appeared as the road wrapped itself around the landscape. For the last kilometre, it disappeared completely, securing its image of isolation.

Private. Solitary. Intimate. Lonely.

Descriptions flowed through Laetitia's thoughts as she shut the car door and looked up from a parking lot overtaken by weeds and time. The connecting path to the lighthouse was winding and cragged. Beyond it, the sun was setting while massive, relentless waves crashed against a mix of sand and stone. It was a spectrum of sound that was novel to her. Novelty was the point of this vacation.

This was Laetitia's first vacation of a rustic, non-tropical variety.

Mexico had been a bit of a bust on her last trip. She had gone out to a giant nightclub only to experience a raid instead of a rave. The masked mob blasted its way in, gunning for the bar's owner and his underground safe room. Laetitia was shot in the leg. Faced with her assailant, she stood, annoyed, and bared her fangs at him. He stiffened and backed away, his eyes wide with fear. It's not like he could report the incident. She considered putting the assailants to rest, but someone would definitely report that.

The siege was clearly a product of organized crime; meanwhile, her own existence was technically criminal. It required a lot of organization already, and more of this was not welcome. She shape-shifted from human to ether on the ravaged dance floor, choosing grey for her morphed colour instead of the technicolour blitz she had experimented with earlier in the evening, and floated back to her hotel. There had been no chance of her death during the raid, of course. But the scar on her leg remained, and continued to piss her off decades later.

She had not fared better at zoos. She visited in the middle of the night, anticipating that some of the animals would react strangely to her, as the pattern of how they responded was still a mystery. Cats generally seemed to like her, dogs were hit and miss, and goats did not approve of her at all. Snakes often slithered beside her as she walked through the woods, but they would not make eye contact. Their company was neither comforting nor stimulating. Sometimes she just wanted to walk in the woods alone.

Rolling the dice on the big cats while visiting the San Diego Zoo one night, she approached the puma's cage. He paced a bit at her arrival outside, then dropped and rolled about on the ground. He looked her straight in the eye, blinking slowly, a big boy cat seeking affection. She leapt over the fence, approached him with caution, and lay down on her side with her back against his belly. It was a warm and beautiful feeling. They breathed together, and she felt better than she had in decades. She turned to face him, relaxed and smiling. Seeing her fangs, he roared and swiped at her face, removing an eye. She roared in return and sank her teeth into his neck. She did not kill him, but his behaviour was permanently altered. The cameras caught nothing but the cat alone, writhing and screaming.

The eye issue was inconvenient, although the scar below the socket was minimal, considering. Laetitia felt herself too young to go without both eyes, so she began taking an eye from her victims. This became a hassle, and she didn't like the smell after a few days. She robbed herself a prosthetic eye and matched the contact lens for the other as closely as possible. The match was always slightly imperfect. Some days she found this attractive, others, repulsive.

Laetitia was inescapably aware that she had no one to talk to about this, or about anything. She experienced her first major depressive episode. She googled depression and other depressing terms until she felt she had self-diagnosed accurately. Neither medication nor therapy seemed like feasible options, and some articles stated that depression could remit on its own, so she chose that route. It was a long five years. She decided that depression was a waste of time, and she devised a relapse prevention plan, which included more vacations.

The seaside dusk was cold. Laetitia buttoned up the wool overcoat that had belonged to one of her brothers. She glided her arms through the straps of a small backpack and began the climb to the lighthouse. The view was unfamiliar to her, pretty. She was pleased.

The structure was very tall up close. Its red and white paint was time-worn and chipped, and the main door was badly rusted along its edge and frame. The windows were translucent, coated with years of sea spray and no maintenance. Laetitia mused about when it was last inhabited, when someone last visited or cared. She looked up and down the building with the thought of scaling it. Her eyes caught the impression of a face in the tiny second floor window. She went still with surprise. The impression dropped out of sight.

Her lighthouse visit was taking an unforeseen turn, which would normally displease her. Today it did not. She decided to confirm the presence and knocked at the corroded steel door. She knocked harder. The banging of her fist against the metal echoed back from the cliff face in between waves. Denial was not an option for the inhabitant.

The door creeped open, revealing the face in more detail. It was that of a young man, late twenties, Laetitia estimated. Good looking. The expression was tentative, then adopted a character of bravery.

"Yes?" he asked. His voice was as lovely as his pale pink face, his pale blue eyes, his black curly hair, his full lips.

"Hi, I'm just … checking out the area," she said, smiling and a bit nervous. The smile came easily. She usually had to remind herself to smile. He stood, unresponsive. "I saw your face in the window and thought I should say hello, or at least let you know I was here, and make sure that's okay?"

"Yeah. Sure. Thank you." He lowered his gaze and began to shut the door.

"But, do you live here?" She took a step forward.

"Yes," he said.

She wasn't convinced. "Are you the lighthouse keeper?"

"Yes."

"I didn't think they had those anymore."

"They do here."

"How long have you been doing that?"

"Oh. A long time." He looked out at the ocean's jagged horizon.

The response seemed dramatic to Laetitia, who engaged in a fair amount of drama on a daily basis as a means of survival. How long had he indeed been there? "You've been doing this a long time? You don't look that old."

"Neither do you," he said. They both smiled.

Laetitia continued. "So … I'm on vacation, and this is my first lighthouse ever. Is there any chance at all I could come in? I've never seen one, and all the others are closed up for the season. I've come a long way. Please. I won't stay long." She turned on the charm at this point. She had been honing this skill since she learned that it would often get her what she wanted—from men, mostly—without killing or terrifying anyone. Charm was still novel to her.

He looked beyond her and then behind him, uncertain but aware that she was unlikely to leave. "A quick run-through," he said. "I keep long hours, so I'm about to retire for the night. Alright?"

"Alright," she said. Her heart, such as it was, raced with excitement.

The inside of the lighthouse was less charming than the outside. It was dark. It smelled of old kerosene fumes and decades of body odour, dust, and damp cement. Some sort of spoiled food, potatoes, perhaps. The furnishings rang temporary: camp bed, camp chair, camp stove, camp lantern. A lumpy black backpack. No pictures, no kitchen table. A misshapen box with some dirty dishes in it.

At a deliberate pace, she walked up the four flights of stairs to the light. The view would have been spectacular if the three-hundred-and-sixty-degree glass had been at all clean. The light spun. It bounced off the dirty glass, it bounced off her translucent chest, and the allure of the tower vanished. She descended to the young man, who had not moved from the middle of his living quarters.

"What's it like to be a lighthouse keeper?" she asked. Is he a lighthouse keeper, she wondered. He looked so young. It was a job for old people, she had imagined. How old was he, really?

"Pretty quiet. I don't do much. But I have to make sure everything works." They stood in silence. "Here's some light," he said, illuminating the camp lantern. "I don't need it myself. I'm used to the dark."

Laetitia's excitement shifted and escalated. She stared intently at his face. "Do you wear contacts?" she asked. She had to work at speaking slowly.

"Sometimes." He cocked his head, surprised by the question. "How did you know?"

"Takes one to know one."

"Hmmm." He looked more deliberately at her eyes. "Yours aren't quite the same colour."

She looked down. "Not quite, no."

"I'm sorry. I didn't mean to make you feel uncomfortable."

His gentle apology thrilled her. It made him even more beautiful.

"What's your name?" she asked, adding quickly, "I'm Laetitia." Laetitia, she heard herself say, surprised. She hadn't used her own name in years. "You?"

He hesitated. "Peter."

"You've been here for how long again?"

"A … long time." He crossed his arms and paced. "I do need to turn in soon."

"Do you?" she asked.

He stopped and shook his head. His face was puzzled by the challenge. "Yes," he laughed. "As I said, I have long days."

"I do, too."

"What do you do?" he asked.

She didn't like the shift. She wanted only to hear the sound of his voice, to watch him talk. "Accountant," she blurted, hoping it would be a boring enough answer to move him along. "How old are you, really?"

"I'm—" the camp lantern expired without warning. The room went into darkness, the last of the sunset glow creating gentle rectangles of light in the windows. "Shit. I'm out of oil, apparently. Shit. I can't get that until tomorrow. Well, this has been a nice visit, thanks for stopping by." She didn't reply. He spun around, his hands reaching out defensively. "Where, where did you go?"

He couldn't see in the dark.

He couldn't see in the dark.

He's not a lighthouse keeper.

He's not a vampire.

Laetitia's disappointment snapped her into a different form, something that occurred when she experienced intolerable levels of emotion. She hovered as a shadow up in the far corner of the cracked ceiling. He had been attractive. He had been kind. He had been near to her age. Or had he? He was not like her, and she was not like him. At all.

She willed herself into human form behind him. "Here," she said, trying not to bare her teeth.

"Yeah." He felt his way toward the creaky metal door, and opened it. Another rectangle of light appeared, large and rough-edged. The space filled with ocean sound. His discomfort was evident, as was the end of their interaction. His voice rose above the waves. "Have a good vacation."

She would not leave until he met her gaze. He wasn't sure what he was looking at, but he saw something beyond her displeasure. She watched as his pretty features shifted into fear. It was a seasoned fear, something this person had lived with a great deal. Then his features transformed into alarm, a sense of danger. He saw her, somehow. She could feel the panic rising from him, and she resented him even more. She hated him for being so disappointingly lovely; she hated herself for being so desperately lonely.

Laetitia stepped out of the lighthouse, and the door shut instantly behind her. The waves were deafening.

She stood for a long time outside the door, her back to the ocean. Her desire to take the squatter was fanatical. She saw his pale blue eyes in her mind, then one pale blue eye. She wished she could have kept this part of him, made it a part of her, without it inevitably rotting in her head. But then his eye wouldn't be pretty anymore. She breathed deeply and managed the decision to leave him be. The ache of having none of him was oppressive. She stood perfectly still outside the door all night, and at first light, she started back down the cliff to her car. She made sure to hover just above the ground as he watched from one of the tiny rectangles.

Notifications

"This is SO our time!" hollered Brianne. She raised her wrist as though rocking out at a concert. A music video sprang to life over the entirety of the ten-by-fourteen wall.

"Dua Lipa!" cried Fann. "Soooo retro!"

"Hahahaha!" laughed Brianne. "That was our time, too. It's always Frianne O'Clock!"

"You didn't, just! You haven't couple-named us in ages."

"Tonight's the night, baby!"

"It's always the night, girl!"

The Party Girls turned Middle-Aged Party Women were in excellent form. They prepared for an evening of cocktails and dancing, or at least cocktails. There was always the hope of picking up prior to dancing, or, otherwise, staying awake long enough for dancing. Their respective daughters had not inherited the party gene, at least not in the sense of living it out face-to-face and flesh-to-flesh. Their daughters were still living at home at age eighteen, studying very different subjects in their mothers' basements. Aimée was absorbed in first year electrical engineering and little else. Jacey was making a serious study of virtual meet-ups and sleeping late. Fann could feel Aimée's annoyance coming up through the floorboards to a greater extent than usual. Earlier, she had told her daughter to zip it, at least for the hour when she and Brianne got ready. She was already preparing herself to receive the blast of disgust on a larger scale if she brought back a guy whose place wasn't an option.

Brianne stopped applying her lipstick. "Newsreel!" she said, more or less, her mouth still in an O-shape.

Nothing changed on the wall. "Newsreel!" chirped Fann. The music video faded behind a scrolling view of her social media feed. Shorts, stills, memes, and a few phrases let them know exactly who was doing what at this moment in time, the who that they cared about, anyway.

"Oh right!" said Brianne, now applying blush. "That guy died."

Fann examined sweater choices. "What guy."

"Him, the one with the super good hair. Didn't you go on some weird date? He was really promising and then really weird?"

The current reel was some sort of memorial, it seemed, with lots of group photos. No one leapt out to Fann. She squinted, puzzled, at the screen. There was good hair, a gentle face. Her eyes and mouth sprung open. "HIM! Him? He died?"

Next, what looked like a family pic. A black woman, two little multiracial girls, lots of smiles.

"What was his name again?"

"We can find out—ah shit"

The reel had moved onto a celeb vacay in the Maldives.

"I can ask the ID—"

"Nah." Fann stood facing the wall, not registering the current images. Her mind and body were busy remembering. "Riiiight!" she said, throwing her head back. "He was awesome, I had thought. It seemed to be totally going somewhere, for both of us, until he came out with this 'personal thing' he wanted to share which could have been ANYTHING except it was dolls and those weird pastel horse things … My Little Pony. That stuff is antique now! Prob worth some dough, maybe I fucked up by finding it too weird, hahahaha."

"You totally blew it!"

"Couldn't handle it. Bolted. Blocked him before I got to the bottom of the stairwell. Too bizarro."

"Yeah."

They switched positions, Fann sitting at the makeup table and Brianne donning the sweater that Fann had selected for herself earlier.

"Maybe you were too hard on the guy, though?" Brianne checked herself out in the little cardi with a self-approving twirl. "Maybe he just liked something unusual? Maybe he is—was—super sweet with those kids? Had a trauma background? At least he wasn't into gonzo porn or fetish WTF."

Gonzo porn and fetish WTF were exactly how a couple of her own dating attempts had ended back in her early 30s. Being a cougar was great. At this age, most guys seemed to hedge their energy and virility bets in the application of fucking and falling asleep over weirdness.

"Disagree," said Fann. "Just weird. Not my thang. Yeesh."

"I hope he found what he needed. Whatever or whoever that was."

Brianne gestured back toward the wall. "She certainly didn't look the type for that. But neither did he, so who knows. It's literally over now, literally."

A guy Fann had met with the goal of intimacy was gone. Dead. A dead almost-lover. It's not like they'd had a relationship. Although in a sense they did, a five-hour platonic one. Fann felt sad and strange. How can you lose someone you never had?

She shook her head, shedding that moment for this one, where Brianne was looking mediocre in the sweater. Wrapping herself in Sweater Plan B, Fann was quite happy with the unsolicited switcheroo. Thanks, darlin', she thought. "N," she muttered, reaching back in time again. "Nick? No. Neil?"

Her wearable chimed a pleasant sound. It was in key with the song, unobtrusive. It chimed again.

"You are rockin' that line with Nike!" proclaimed Brianne. Drinks on you, she thought.

Fann nodded. "Reppin' it pretty good. Who knew cougar-print track suits would make ME money with friggin' Nike?? Hahahaha. I LOVE this." She looked down at the updated commission stats coming through. She might even buy a round tonight. "Funny, they're such a big hit with the late teen set instead of the 45 to 55 test market."

"Who cares?" Brianne wrapped her arms around her friend's shoulders from behind. "Mirror, Mirror!" The wall became a digital mirror of the pair, smiling at their larger-than-life selves ready for town. The wall took a selfie and posted it. "Ping Caropolis!" said Brianne, reaching for her purse. "End Reel."

A music video, now featuring a contemporary artist, filled the wall. The faces of a hundred shaved-headed women of diverse backgrounds sang a millisecond behind each other where the faces of Fann and Brianne were cast seconds ago, fading in and out over the faces of people around the world here and gone just seconds before that, tied by connection that was illusory and real, impossible and possible, and possibly illusory again.

Truth's Bedrooms of the Heart

We move from room to room at each stay.

We move from room to room in sequence, entwined with whom we have invited.

The door opens, we collapse into the upper right chamber. Our forms are weary, bruised, spent. Sometimes angry, annoyed, distant. We float and pulsate, we need rest. But here is where the stay is short. We pull the heart-strings to close the blinds. All we want is sleep. The door opens,

we fall into the lower left chamber. More light, there is more light glowing. In the deep red flow of the walls, we notice subtle patterns and designs. We are given towels and bathrobes, the promise of comfort and cleanliness, renewal. We wonder in silence: will the shower be warm, will the tub be deep, the tub deep, tub deep. We drop down the tubular corridor, drop down into the angel lungs

We burst apart!

We burst apart into billions of tiny crimson cells of light and we sail and fly and bounce and crash into exquisite parts of ourselves and each other. We mix, we divide, we divine, the ride, the ride dizzy, dizzying, invigorating, disorienting, euphoric, disorganized until we are

> suddenly aligned. We have form. The angel lungs have reformed and released us into the upper left chamber. We are naked in a place so explosively bright. The décor is entirely absent of reason. We see each other as though for the very first time. Everything is electric and we are beautiful. We rush into each other in a rush to feel the rush just that much greater. We think of nothing until the heartstrings tighten

pulling open the hatch between rooms. We are unable to fathom how it is too much, the sublime takes more than it gives. How quickly it is that we lose purpose while losing our purpose, how far this is beyond us. No one is to linger in the upper left chamber. We would never ever move on from here

on our own terms but as it turns

> the music is indeed alluring in the lower left chamber. The music of fun in the afternoon, the place we prepare to go out. We have time here to dress. We choose from millions of masks and costumes and thoughts, auras, voices, demeanours, and poses. There is a curio clock on the wall. Its face has many hours and movements at varying speeds, counting something down. Counting something down some down, son down, sundown.

> We are flowing toward the exit now we are not ready often or sometimes we are not ready

> our being is born of giving. We are driven to give, it is in fact backward from how we think. We believe we go out to consume, to drink in, in time to consume all of time when in truth, we put one foot in front and one moment behind the other. Our chests,

our faces flow forward and open in and out, the blood it goes in and out, sometimes we separate and cannot find each other by choice, sometimes not so much until

we collapse back inside the first room, entwined with whom we have invited.

Where we are not ready often and sometimes not ready.

There are times of electrical storms and events that rock all of the chambers. We may not feel safe but we are safer here than anywhere else. There is no ease or rest in nesting or reviving. In flashes of light we see cracks in the walls. During this stay, this time, the rhythm unstable, the space and circuits of each room disrupted. In the lower left chamber, we still try to dance. But it is tiring, not knowing the time or the rhythm, the time of the rhythm changing all of the time. We hit into each other in ways not as loving. We enter here thin, we exit then thinner.

The music stops. The light opens and fills

the chamber we occupy now singular, whole. we do not rush between rooms, between wars, between worlds. there is nothing separate or separated. here, the angel lungs hold us all of the time. we feel the odd bump, hear the odd muffled sound from far and away and outside. we are warm and still and stronger together, become stronger here in the river where we float and dream as a new set of chambers begins to form within and become us, for as long as that may ever be

this is all we have, the all we know

this is all we know

for Dad (1936 – 2021).

Acknowledgements

Thank you to those who read and provided encouragement around the first book. This one exists because of you.

The early readers are the first to lay eyes on what happened in my mind and then on paper. They were kind enough to give of their time, perspectives, expertise, and themselves. I cannot truly convey their impact. Un énorme merci, a profound thank you to Rhonda Whittaker, Sylvie V. LeBlanc, Shaun LeBlanc, and Michelle Jay.

I am grateful for Tanya Davis's finesse and openness in her copyediting process. The book's silent strength rests on it.

Sasha, who turned 18 the year I finished writing this book, sat on my pages a lot. She otherwise napped or watched Kitty TV from various windows of the house. I deleted, then reinstated this paragraph several times. She belongs here.

Thank you to Natasha LeBlanc, Megan Livingstone, Wendy Mills, Jamie Berry, Sophie Auffrey, and Jean-François Tremblay. Thank you to the musical artists with whom I work and play. This may be a different medium, but you are here.

For Mardie Ettles, thank you for being proud of me. Sorry for all the swearing.

Michelle is much more than an early reader. She is a vibrant, sensitive, responsive soul. Her gentle, yet tidal force of love and encouragement fills the space between these words.

About the Author

Robin Anne Ettles is a multidisciplinary artist originally from Amiskwacîwâskahikan (Edmonton) who calls Epekwitk (Prince Edward Island) home. As a freelance bassist and guitarist, she has toured parts of North America, Europe, and Australia, and continues to accompany artists of different genres. She completed her master's studies in clinical psychology at l'Université de Moncton. This is Robin's second book of short stories. The first won the Rubery Book Award for Short Stories in 2020.

• The Last Supperware (♡ this title!) This story is missing...
a lot. Debra isn't part of the event that spurs the
climax (Jess drunk, knocks Tupperware off table, Debra
runs upstairs to take back stolen ~~swim cap~~ and saucy Jess swim cap). And how does
the trans-woman party leader play in? As is, Debra just
gawks at her, fascinated. *coincidence can get one into, not
                                              out of predicament

• SB Daniel observes his grotesque neighbour. Upon observing
another, he realizes he's becoming them.

• Dear Brenda — an email exchange about bees and
pesticides btw neighbours is combative then apologetic when
Brenda disappears from the block and her email. Turns out
she was an environmentalist but an adulterous schmuck.
I like this one.

• Rolfie — unnamed protag visits friend who is catatonic in a
heatwave. Best friend. Chose sister. Who won't (can't) rouse herself
for even a greeting. Meanwhile, protag w/ tragic childhood (turned
out so well). (Yep. I know the type) "Look how well I turned out"

* Critical — a restaurant review (from a pretentious ~~town~~ world famous boo)
Hilarious food combinations and observations including erudite
(p 27) seafood desserts (like Travis' oysters and chocolate!)
Having written a scathing rebuke of a new restaurant in his old
hometown, D'Arcy soon finds "The intersection of his past and
           Sinclair
current lives was unbearable" (his review will destroy jobs,
even the town... think me eviscerating Swift Current, just cuz I
reaches for relevance). — Should've ended, perhaps, 1 paragraph
after the editor's revised review. Everything is contained in that.

• Dream Estate — Before, during, after an earthquake on the 39th
floor, Karina's sleep dreams follow her through waking life.
Kind of like visual, hallucinatory ADHD, where she has to mask to
be in the NT world.

• Reconstructionism — Jason attends the death scene of a woman
@ a beach. A painter, he reconstructs crime scenes on canvas for this
one, his own arm appears in the painting (his anorak).

• under the same moon — Deshawn spends three nights alone
at a broken-down theme park before her wedding. Why did her
wedding party choose this? Now she's paranoid about her fiancée (sort
of). Was that the point?
          —Ah! Okay. Next story is about Noah's (fiancée) experience

Printed in Canada